Caleb couldn't help noticing that Nadine's hands were shaking, but he stifled the urge to take her hand in his in an effort to comfort her and show his support. Getting this recording was the important thing at the moment.

Fortunately, Caleb had several investigators who did work, like Nadine's background check, for him, Morgan and the True Foundation. Discovering his father's deception had taught him not to take anything at face value.

The moment he set down his phone near Nadine's, the eerie voice crackled as he issued a threat to her.

"You were warned to stop sticking your nose where it doesn't belong. Now you're going to have to face the consequences for doing that."

And then the line went dead.

* * *

The Coltons of Colorado: Love, danger and redemption are in store for this family

Dear Reader,

Just when you thought that the Coltons had finally run out of families, they pull you back in with a story that is sure to spark your imagination. Back in the day, Ben Colton married his childhood sweetheart, Isadora, and they promptly went to work creating Colton babies. This new batch of Coltons were all honorable people who, thanks to their father, who became a judge, lived very well. A little too well, it turned out, because the honorable judge was not as honorable as his family had thought. When his dealings finally came to light, he was thrown off the bench and arrested. But before he could be brought to trial, Ben Colton was in a car accident that cost him his life.

Led by the eldest Colton siblings, Caleb and his twin sister, Morgan, the family proceeded to restore the Colton name and take on the fight for wrongly convicted so-called felons. Being the champion for the downtrodden cost Caleb his first marriage, but it did lead him to take up Nadine Sutherland's fight against Rutledge Oil. According to Nadine, an activist of the first water, the oil company had tricked her father into signing away his land and the oil rights that went with it. And now someone is following her, determined to get rid of this crusader before she can cause any real trouble.

Want to see how this turns out?

As always, I thank you for picking up one of my books to read and from the bottom of my heart, I wish you someone to love who loves you back.

Love,

Marie Ferrarella

COLTON'S PURSUIT OF JUSTICE

Marie Ferrarella

HARLEQUIN
ROMANTIC SUSPENSE

Special thanks and acknowledgment are given to Marie Ferrarella for her contribution to the The Coltons of Colorado miniseries.

Recycling programs for this product may not exist in your area.

ISBN-13: 978-1-335-75957-3

Colton's Pursuit of Justice

Copyright © 2022 by Harlequin Books S.A.

This edition published by arrangement with Harlequin Books S.A.

For questions and comments about the quality of this book, please contact us at CustomerService@Harlequin.com.

Harlequin Enterprises ULC
22 Adelaide St. West, 40th Floor
Toronto, Ontario M5H 4E3, Canada
www.Harlequin.com

Printed in U.S.A.

USA TODAY bestselling and RITA® Award–winning author **Marie Ferrarella** has written more than two hundred and fifty books for Harlequin, some under the name Marie Nicole. Her romances are beloved by fans worldwide. Visit her website, marieferrarella.com.

Books by Marie Ferrarella

Harlequin Romantic Suspense

The Coltons of Colorado

Colton's Pursuit of Justice

Colton 011: Chicago

Colton 911: The Secret Network
Colton 911: Secret Defender

The Coltons of Kansas

Exposing Colton Secrets

The Coltons of Mustang Valley

Colton Baby Conspiracy

Cavanaugh Justice

A Widow's Guilty Secret
Cavanaugh's Surrender
Cavanaugh Rules
Cavanaugh's Bodyguard
Cavanaugh Fortune
How to Seduce a Cavanaugh
Cavanaugh or Death
Cavanaugh Cold Case
Cavanaugh in the Rough

Visit the Author Profile page at Harlequin.com for more titles.

To

Tiffany & Edy Melgar,

And

Their Fantastic Little Girls,

Elliana & Adelyn.

Rays of Sunshine Do Not Come Any Brighter.

Love,

G-Mama

Chapter 1

Funny how thoughts can suddenly sneak up on a person out of the blue, Caleb Colton couldn't help thinking. One minute, he was letting himself into his riverfront penthouse condo, feeling far wearier than his thirty-nine years actually warranted. The next minute, it had suddenly hit him that a major anniversary was coming up soon.

Twenty years since his father, the former Judge Benjamin Colton, had died in a tragic car accident when his vehicle had fatally slid on a stretch of icy road.

Closing the door behind him, Caleb stood there

in the dark penthouse, waiting for at least a shred of emotion to slam into him.

It didn't.

There was a time when he wouldn't have believed that he could be this removed from such a life-altering event. After all, his had always been such a close-knit family. But that was before his father, a much sought-after guest at the most exclusive social gatherings, had dragged the family name through the mud with his secret dealings.

And for what? For money.

The knowledge left him feeling hollow.

During his last decade on the bench, his father took kickbacks from private-prison owners and juvenile-detention-facility owners. In exchange for these secret payments, Ben Colton sentenced an increasing number of adults and teenagers to those selected facilities.

And for a while, Caleb recalled, no one seemed to be aware of what was actually happening. On the surface, everything seemed to be going well. As a result, there was money for everything: fine clothing, a lavish lifestyle, a huge house in an up-and-coming neighborhood in Blue Larkspur, Colorado.

In short, there was more than enough money for everything he and his eleven brothers and sisters could have ever wanted.

As far as he knew, the family all believed they

were able to live this kind of life thanks to their father's inheritance—until it was brought to light by an enterprising investigative reporter that there *was* no such inheritance.

The source of the money—all of it—was from bribes he pocketed.

Caleb poured himself a glass of ginger ale. He was far too exhausted to drink any alcoholic beverage at this hour. It would instantly knock him out on his feet.

Sitting down in the dimly lit living room, he raised his glass to his father's memory in a mock toast.

"Why did you do it, Dad? You were smart enough to know better. You certainly should have known it couldn't have lasted. You threw away our good name and your reputation for things that in the final analysis had no real intrinsic value. And worse than that," he added with a trace of restrained anger, "you broke Mom's heart.

"But she stood by you despite all that." Caleb laughed softly to himself as memories insisted on flooding his brain. "We all did. And then you died," he concluded, "leaving the rest of us to clean up your mess.

"It took us twenty years, Dad, but we did it. We are working on making restitution to all those people who were made to suffer thanks to you. Because of the Truth Foundation that Morgan and I, as attorneys, set up, we managed to exonerate each and every one of the people you wrongfully imprisoned or gave overly harsh sentences to so that your pals could keep them in their private institutions that much longer.

"Funny thing is," Caleb said as he took another sip from his glass, "I know that in a very odd way, you did it all out of love.

"But the money never meant that much to any of us. Trust me, we would have all been a lot happier poorer—as long as the family's integrity remained intact."

Caleb sighed as he set the glass down on the coffee table. After a moment, he pulled himself up to his feet. He *really* needed to get to bed, he thought. He was putting in far too much time at his office and at the Foundation. His workaholic nature had wound up killing his marriage years ago, and if he wasn't careful, it would eventually wind up killing him, too.

"Too bad you never thought to ask any of us if we would have minded being poorer," Caleb murmured under his breath as he made his way up the stairs. A sad smile twisted his lips. "Especially Mom." Ever since his father had dropped that awful, soul-jarring bombshell that he was being arrested for being on the take, it had upended all of their lives. As the oldest—by ten minutes, thanks to being born ahead of his twin sister—Caleb had felt an overpowering need to be there for his mother and his siblings and to somehow right the wrong that had been done.

Even now, Caleb still felt that same sense of responsibility. That need to be there for everyone in every capacity was what had ultimately brought about the end of his marriage to his college sweetheart. For all intents and purposes, their union had suffered an untimely death before it was even five years old.

Over the years, two more long-term relationships he was in came to an end for the same reason. What he felt was his calling took precedence over any sort of romantic relationship. Because of that, at this point, Caleb had resigned himself to remaining single for the rest of his life.

Heaven knew he had enough things to fill up his world that required his attention, what with helping head up the law firm of Colton and Colton, and his family. And, if all that wasn't enough, there was the Truth Foundation. He and Morgan had put the organization together to try to atone for some of their father's transgressions by helping the wrongfully convicted overturn their sentences.

This morning, the first thing on his agenda before his day officially began was to swing by his mother's house. He wanted to make sure that she was doing all right.

To him, Isadora Colton was nothing short of completely incredible. When the truth about what Ben Colton was doing suddenly came to light and their whole well-ordered world just blew apart, his mother had never complained, not even once. Despite the glaring subterfuge and the humiliation it generated when the general population became aware of it, she never wavered, never stopped loving the man she had married, the father of her twelve children.

An ironic smile curved Caleb's lips. That old country-and-western classic about standing by her man could have been written about his mother, he thought. Considering what she had gone through, the woman looked amazingly youthful. Had to be good genes, he thought. There was no other explanation.

Caleb rang the doorbell to the house where they had all grown up before letting himself in. Absently, he pocketed his key.

"Are you up, Mom?" he called out, knowing full well that she was. She had always been an early riser. He couldn't remember a day when she had remained in bed past 7:00 a.m., even on weekends.

Usually, she was up before then.

"In the kitchen, dear," Isa called out. The youthful-looking blonde beamed at her oldest born as he walked into the kitchen. "To what do I owe this un-expected surprise?" she asked Caleb, then tilted her head in his direction, enabling her eldest to brush a kiss against her cheek.

"I just wanted to see how you were doing, Mom," he told her, doing his best to sound cheerful and nonchalant.

"I'm doing just fine, Caleb," his mother answered honestly. Turning from the stove and the breakfast she was preparing, the light suddenly dawned on her. Isa fixed her oldest son with a knowing look. "This is because of that awful anniversary that's coming up, isn't it?" she asked, knowing full well that that had to be why he was checking up on her.

In her opinion, Caleb's furrowed brow gave him away. Of all her children, she knew that her oldest son had taken his father's betrayal the hardest.

Caleb laughed softly to himself, shaking his head. "I could never put anything over on you, Mom."

"Why would you want to, dear?" Isa wanted to know. "It's always best to be honest," she told Caleb, repeating the sentiment that, for the last two decades, she had insisted govern all of their lives. "Remember," she underscored. "No secrets. *Ever.*"

"I'm a lawyer, Mom," he needlessly reminded her. "That could make things a wee bit rough when it comes to matters of attorney-client privilege."

Isa inclined her head. "Challenging, perhaps," she agreed. "But not impossible. Here, eat something," she said, placing the platter she had just finished preparing in front of where her son usually sat instead of her own place setting.

"Isn't that supposed to be your breakfast?" he protested.

Isa waved away her son's words. "No, it's yours," she informed him as if it was a foregone conclusion.

Caleb leveled a look at her as he attempted to push the plate back to its rightful place—in front of her chair. "You couldn't possibly have known I was coming over."

Isa's eyes narrowed ever so slightly as she gave him a penetrating look. "Couldn't have I?" she questioned in a manner that effectively contradicted his protest. "Don't argue with your mother, Caleb. I know everything." She moved the plate back in front of him. "Now, eat."

Experience told him that he would save himself a lot of time, not to mention effort, if he just went along with what his mother had just said. Besides, it wasn't as if there was only one serving of food available in the spacious house. Thanks to the inheritance that his maternal grandparents had left her and an inborn knack for frugality, it could be maintained that after everything was said and done, Isa Colton was doing quite well.

Isa flashed her son a warm, broad smile as Caleb finally took his seat at the spacious kitchen counter that had been part of the extensive renovations that her children had gifted her with for her sixtieth birthday.

Isa sat right next to him, nursing the cup of coffee that she had poured for herself earlier.

"This is nice," she commented about his taking his breakfast beside her. "Like the old days."

Isa refrained from saying anything further on the subject, feeling that it might cause Caleb to reflect more deeply and that could only stir up unwanted memories.

"Can I get you some coffee?" she offered, beginning to rise again.

Caleb placed his hand over hers, stopping her before she was on her feet. "No thanks, Mom. I'll have enough coffee over the course of the day to sink a battleship. Maybe even two battleships." He nodded at the breakfast plate before him. "This is good."

"It's simple," Isa pointed out. She knew better than to pretend to be an excellent cook. Isa was aware of her limitations. She smiled at her son. "I could always do simple."

Caleb sighed as he shook his head. Some things never changed. In a way, he found that rather comforting. "You've got to learn how to take a compliment."

Isa pretended to look surprised. "I thought that was what I was doing," she said with a straight face.

Ingrained habit had him glancing at his watch. It was getting late, he realized. There were papers at the office he just remembered he needed to sign.

Finishing the rest of the reassigned eggs and toast quickly, Caleb wiped his mouth and then deposited his napkin on the plate. He began to take his plate to the sink, but this time it was his mother's turn to stop him.

"I'll take care of that," Isa told him.

Caleb relented, then asked her again, "You're sure you're all right?" He wanted to double-check that she actually was. His father's death was twenty years in the past, but it still had a way of burrowing in and upending their lives when they least expected it.

Isa patted her son's cheek. "I couldn't be better, darling," she assured him. "Really," she underscored. "Why wouldn't I be? My son just stopped by to have breakfast with me."

Caleb laughed, amused. "It doesn't take much to satisfy you, does it, Mom?"

Isa's eyes twinkled. "That's what I've been telling you all along, dear," she said. She rose from the counter at the same time that Caleb did.

"What are you doing?" he asked when his mother fell into step beside him.

"Why, I'm walking you to the front door," she replied matter-of-factly.

"I know where the front door is, Mom," Caleb said with a laugh. "I've used it often enough."

"I know," she replied. "But walking you to it gives me a few more moments to savor your presence. We mothers can be greedy that way," she informed him with a smile that was nothing short of charming.

As he stopped by the front door, Caleb took his mother's hands in his. She had made it sound as if this was a rare visit on his part instead of quite the opposite.

"I was just here a few days ago," he reminded her.

"I know," she answered. "But I don't take anything for granted anymore, you know that."

Despite the smile curving her lips, his mother was very serious. Caleb knew what she was referring to.

His father had done that to her, Caleb couldn't help thinking. Ben Colton's deceptions had done that to all of them, robbed each and every one of them of that all-important gift they had once been born with: trust.

Luckily, that hadn't affected the family dynamic.

But it very well could have, Caleb thought. It could have made them suspicious of everything someone else did from that long-ago day forward.

Caleb lingered for a moment, holding his mother's hands in his.

"Well, if anything changes, you know where to find me," he told her, giving her a quick kiss good-bye.

"Yes, I do, Caleb. And I know where to find you even if *nothing* changes," Isa assured her son with a chuckle.

About to leave, Caleb looked at his mother over

his shoulder. Impulsively, he added, "I'll swing by tomorrow morning," and then he was gone.

Because of the unusual lack of traffic that morning, Caleb arrived at work quickly. Once upon a time, before his father had sold out his integrity—and *before* he was appointed judge—this had been his office.

Caleb could remember how impressed he had been when he'd first walked into it.

The space had seemed a great deal bigger to him back then, but he had been about five or six and easily impressed by everything—especially by his father, he recalled. The man had seemed like a giant to him, as if he was at least ten feet tall.

Too bad he'd had to learn otherwise, Caleb thought, parking his car in his usual space and getting out.

It appeared that Morgan was already there, he noted. Her car was parked right next to his.

Caleb walked inside, telling himself he needed to shake this oppressive feeling that had descended over him. He had work to get to and he couldn't waste time mentally floundering around in the past. Dwelling on it would change nothing. He and Morgan had spent almost the last decade trying very hard to make up for his father's terrible misdeeds and offenses, to restore the lives that had been so badly damaged by their father's actions.

"Hi," Caleb said by way of a greeting. "Did I miss

anything?" he asked, referring to the fact that she had gotten to the office ahead of him and their assistants.

"Yes, Annie called," Morgan answered, stopping him dead in his tracks.

"Annie?" he repeated, surprised.

"Yes. Annie." Morgan glanced up for a second. "Your ex-wife."

"I know who Annie is," Caleb answered, slightly annoyed by his twin's attitude. Why was Annie calling him at the office? "Did she say what she wanted?"

"Yes," Morgan answered, obviously preoccupied. "For you to call her back."

Caleb pressed his lips together, trying to be patient. "You are a regular fount of information this morning."

"I do my best," Morgan answered cheerfully before looking back at the brief she was working on.

"Seriously, did she give any indication why she was calling me so early in the day?" *Or at all?* he added silently.

"Haven't a clue," Morgan replied, thumbing through the pages on her desk. And then she paused for a moment to look up from the brief she was reviewing. "Maybe she wanted to give the two of you another chance."

Yeah, right, he thought. That ship had sailed a long while ago.

"I don't think that would exactly sit too well with her husband and their three kids," Caleb quipped.

Morgan got back to work again. "You're probably right. I guess you're just going to have to call her and put that question to her yourself."

Caleb nodded, more to himself than to his twin. "I guess so," he murmured.

Morgan looked up just as he was leaving her office to go into his own. "I wrote the number down if you need it," she told him, holding up a Post-it note.

"I have it," he answered.

His ex-wife's situation had changed since they had been together but very little else had, including her phone number.

Caleb couldn't help wondering what was up. His and Annie's divorce had been amicable enough. He had even sent a wedding gift when she went on to marry Pete Jackson, a man who, unlike him, could give her the time she more than deserved.

But Caleb truthfully couldn't remember when she'd called him. Since the divorce, they didn't exactly get together all that much.

Any other woman might have held what had come to pass against him. Rather than put her or at least their marriage first, he had immersed himself in his family and in trying to right the wrongs his father had committed. Restoring family honor became all-important to him.

Sadly, Annie and their marriage had somehow gotten lost in the shuffle, falling by the wayside until he had a little free time to devote to her and to it.

For some reason, while he made all these excuses to himself about why he was too busy to come home, he'd felt that Annie would understand, that she was all right with this crusade he had undertaken, the crusade that had all but consumed his soul.

He should have known better.

Even a saint would have had trouble adjusting to the situation, and Annie was still a flesh-and-blood woman who had every right to expect her husband to be there for her rather than always rushing off like some self-appointed superhero.

He got out Annie's number and stared at it for a long moment.

He hadn't a clue what had prompted her to call him today, but he was determined not to let her down, no matter what she was going to ask him to do.

When Caleb heard the phone on the other end begin ringing, he braced himself.

Chapter 2

"Hello?"

The moment he heard Annie's voice against his ear, Caleb felt as if he had instantly been thrown back into another era.

It took him a second or two to get his bearings and remind himself that Annie was no longer his college sweetheart or his wife. She was now Pete Jackson's wife and the happy, fulfilled mother of Pete's children. Annie, he knew, made a wonderful mother.

Everything was as it should be—for her. That it wasn't for him, well, Caleb thought, he had no one to blame for that but himself.

"Annie, it's Caleb," he told her needlessly. "Morgan said that you called and wanted to speak to me."

"I did, and I do," she answered.

He could have sworn that Annie was stalling. He would even say that she sounded nervous. That was highly unusual for the normally self-assured woman. Whatever had prompted Annie to call had obviously undermined her confidence.

He immediately wondered what was wrong.

Since Annie didn't say anything further to cast light on the situation, Caleb decided to try to coax the information out of her.

"About?" he pressed.

He heard her take in a deep breath. "It's about my cousin," she finally said, the words coming out slowly.

He thought for a moment, but no image came to mind to correspond with the word *cousin*.

"I'm sorry, Annie," he apologized. "But I'm drawing a blank." Caleb moved the pile of papers on his desk closer to him. He needed to get started signing these things, he reminded himself.

"My cousin Nadine," Annie said, her tone indicating that she obviously expected him to remember the woman. "You met her at the big Christmas party my family threw that first year we were married." The long-ago memory appeared to stir something within her as Annie sighed. "That was a long time ago, and

I guess I shouldn't really expect you to remember," she admitted. "But you *did* meet her."

He was still coming up empty. "I'll take your word for it," Caleb said. Just because he couldn't remember—another testament to the fact that he had never devoted enough time to Annie when they were married, he thought—didn't mean that it hadn't taken place. "Anyway, moving on. What about Nadine?" he asked, trying to prod the conversation along.

"I was talking to her last night and she needs help."

"Legal help?" Caleb guessed, thinking that had to be the reason why Annie had thought of him and not someone else.

"Among other things."

Caleb stopped signing papers and gave the phone conversation his full attention. "What other things?"

He heard Annie sigh again. "It's kind of complicated," she told him. "I should let Nadine tell you all this herself."

"Do I even get a hint?" he wanted to know.

He could tell Annie was wrestling with herself—and then she finally said, "Suffice to say that Nadine feels that someone is after her."

"Feelings of persecution?" he guessed.

"No, these aren't feelings of persecution," Annie insisted. "'Feelings' don't send warning emails or make threatening phone calls. If Nadine thinks that someone is actually following her—she mentioned a sedan—then I'd bet big money that she is right. And that it has something to do with her father, my uncle Al. As I recall, the oil company displayed interest in his fracking rights." Her tone changed to one of supplication as she qualified, "Would you look into it for her, Caleb? After work. For me?"

Back when they were married, there had been so many things, things he could have attended to but hadn't because something else had taken precedence.

How could he justify turning his back on her now?

"It would have to be after six," he told Annie. "Would your cousin be all right with that?"

"Absolutely. After six would be fine." Caleb could all but hear the smile in her voice. "Should Nadine come to your office, or—?"

He nodded, then realized that of course Annie couldn't see him. "The office would be great," he assured her. "Could you call her and give her the directions?"

"Sure. They're tattooed on my heart," she said dryly, adding, "I'm sorry, you're going out of your way to do me a favor and I'm being sarcastic."

Because she had apologized so quickly, Caleb gave her a pass. "It's not like I don't have it coming, Annie. If that's the worst thing you've got, I'd say I'm getting off pretty easy. So, is it settled? You'll call your cousin and ask her to meet me in my office so we can discuss whoever's after her and why."

She evidently caught the slight note of skepticism in Caleb's voice. "My cousin doesn't make things up, Caleb."

"I didn't say she did," he answered, closing the door to that subject. Switching gears, Caleb asked, "Is your cousin's last name the same as yours was?"

"Yes. Sutherland," she said for good measure. "Why? Is that a problem?" Annie queried.

He wanted to look into the woman, but he felt it wouldn't be tactful to say as much to his ex, at least for now. "No, I just want to keep everything organized for Rebekah."

"Rebekah?" Annie questioned, slightly confused.

"Rebekah Hanlan, the assistant that Morgan and I share," he told Annie. "Rebekah's a stickler when it comes to following rules. She's going to want to know what name to fill in on the schedule," he explained.

"Just so you know, the basis of the issue is that her dad, my uncle Al, who has the beginnings of dementia, signed over the fracking rights to his land to Rutledge Oil. Nadine thinks he was coerced and she's trying to prove it. The phone calls and other stuff started after that."

"Anything else?"

"No," Annie answered cheerfully. "I'm good."

"Yes, you are," Caleb freely admitted.

He owed her, Caleb thought. Big-time. The fact that she had turned her life around and was happy with the way it had had worked out didn't change any of that. If helping her cousin out helped to balance the scales between them a little, well, so much the better.

"Your cousin will come to the office at six?"

"Six-*ish*," Annie corrected.

"Six-ish?" Caleb repeated quizzically.

Annie laughed softly in acknowledgment. "Nadine has a habit of running late at times," she explained. "I just don't want you to think she's forgotten your meeting if she arrives at the office a few minutes after the appointed time. I know how much you appreciate punctuality."

"I'll cut her some slack if she gets here late—as long as it's not *too* late," he qualified.

"Duly noted," Annie told him. "And, Caleb?"

He was just about to terminate the call and stopped. "Yes?"

"Thank you."

Caleb smiled to himself. No doubt about it, he liked being on the same wavelength as Annie. There was a time—it seemed like eons ago now—that had been the norm.

"Don't mention it," he responded.

As he hung up, he tried to remember what this

cousin-in-need looked like. Still failing, he decided to go another route and look the woman up on social media.

He came across various references to Nadine participating in, and getting arrested at, protest demonstrations. The woman, he decided after scanning one story after another, turned out to be quite a crusader.

Caleb glanced at the pile of unsigned papers that were still on his desk. They were his priority.

But then his curiosity got the better of him.

How long could verifying information regarding Annie's cousin take him? Besides, he thought, he never liked coming into a meeting, *any* sort of a meeting, unprepared.

Maybe he would even be able to find enough to help him tactfully tell Annie that she should distance herself from this so-called activist before it wound up getting her into trouble as well.

At least it was worth a shot, he thought as he began his research into Nadine.

She had been at it for over an hour.

Nadine Sutherland had given up trying to concentrate on fashioning the earrings she had set out to create for her client. The inspiration just wasn't coming.

She had learned a long time ago that in order to

be successful, she had to be entirely focused on the job at hand, and right now, all she could think of was how angry she was with Rutledge Oil for taking advantage of her father.

She could feel a tightness forming in her chest whenever she thought about it.

Didn't the people there have *any* sort of a moral conscience at all?

Al Sutherland was a man who was getting on in years. Worse than that, he was verging on full-blown dementia. He couldn't have realized what he was doing when they talked him into signing over his property rights. Property rights that allowed the oil company to gain all the fracking rights over his land.

Another wave of anger washed over her.

How could anyone do such a thing? she silently demanded for what felt like the thousandth time. And, growing dementia or not, how could her father have agreed to doing something so life-altering without even *trying* to consult her?

Or at least someone in the family?

The answer was that he obviously hadn't known what he was doing. Although, heaven knew, her father was not about to admit to doing something so irresponsible and, let's face it, she thought, downright foolish. That would point to the fact that her father *hadn't* been in his right mind, at least not at the time when he had agreed to relinquish his rights.

And, despite an intense search on her part, Nadine was not able to find any sort of indication that any money had exchanged hands to solidify this deal. What that meant, as far as she could see, was that the oil company was actually guilty of stealing fracking rights to this land from her father.

Plain and simple, Rutledge Oil had duped him.

Not that her father would ever admit to anything like that happening.

It seemed like the less control he actually exhibited over his actions and thoughts, the more her father would lash out at her or at anyone else who might even remotely suggest that this land rights "transfer" had been done in an increasingly frequent moment of complete confusion.

Her father would rather die than admit to the steady encroachment of debilitating dementia.

Nadine sighed, frustrated. She pushed aside the incomplete earrings that refused to take shape despite her best intentions. She felt really worn out.

Of all the causes she had ever championed, all the reasons she had put herself out there, holding up signs and attempting to secure the public's attention for one purpose or another, this was by far the fight that was the most personal to her.

The one that counted above all the others.

And the one she felt doomed to lose if something didn't finally turn her way.

Which was why she had finally put aside her stubborn pride and turned to her cousin Annie for help. And it wasn't just because this was a family matter.

It was a fight that appeared as if it involved her very safety as well. She'd investigated to the point that she had obviously not just rattled someone's cage but had gotten that "someone"—apparently Rutledge Oil, or at least someone *in* there—very angry as well.

Apparently, that "someone" within the oil company was determined to turn the tables on her and exact revenge for her interference. Right now, she could only assume the kind of form that "revenge" might take.

But a sinking feeling in her stomach told her that she already knew. She had heard stories about the oil company intimidating people—or worse. There were several people who dared to challenge them and suddenly disappeared.

There were times when she really longed for the simple life when she didn't have to worry about what tomorrow might bring.

But then, Nadine reminded herself, a life like that would be extremely boring to someone of her nature and, more importantly, someone with her drive. Besides, people needed to have someone stand up for them, and she was willing to take on that position.

Still, Nadine mused, looking back at the earrings that refused to come to life, right about now, there was something to be said for "boring."

At that moment, as she lost herself in thought, the phone rang.

Chapter 3

Nadine could feel her heart pounding. Hard. It took a few moments for it to resume a normal beat. These days, what with the threatening emails, the nasty phone calls, not to mention the hang-ups and having to suddenly look over her shoulder, positive that there was someone following her, intent on harming her, Nadine's heart had hardly had a chance to resume a normal rhythm in weeks. She would have gone to the police, but she knew they would turn a deaf ear because she was an activist and thus a troublemaker in their book.

She almost didn't answer the phone. But, she reasoned, that would be cowardly. In essence, that would be letting the other side know that they had succeeded in intimidating her, and she absolutely refused to do that. Nadine was not about to quietly fade into the woodwork and let the bullies win. She could never live with herself. She spent her life protesting corporate bullies and promoting causes supporting the less fortunate, and she wasn't going to give in now.

Summoning her anger to her, Nadine cloaked herself in it and jerked up the receiver on her old landline.

"Hello?" she all but barked.

"Nadine? Is that you?" Annie questioned. Her cousin didn't usually sound this way, concern instantly evident. "Is everything all right?"

Hearing a familiar voice, Nadine exhaled, letting the breath out as quietly as she could. She waited for her heart to settle down. Again.

"Sorry, I didn't mean to shout, Annie. I wasn't expecting to hear your voice on the other end of the line."

Annie didn't need any further explanation. "They've been bothering you again, haven't they, Nadine?"

There was no need for Annie to elaborate any further. Both she and Nadine knew exactly who "they" were.

"Once or twice," Nadine replied elusively.

She wasn't about to go into any further details. She didn't want to worry her cousin any more than she already had when she asked Annie for her help in the first place.

"Well, I think you can stop worrying soon. I called up my ex, Caleb Colton, about your problem and he said that he can meet you at his office after work. That'll be around six, or a little later, if that's all right with you," Annie told her.

Nadine felt a sense of relief but thought that maybe she was being overoptimistic. She thought that she would be used to it by now. She had lost count of the number of times she had been disappointed when it came to things that she had championed. Organizations she wanted to make changes never kept their word. People or corporations with power should put others' needs ahead of their own, she felt, and she was sure Caleb would be no different.

Still, she appreciated her cousin's effort. And who knew, maybe Caleb could actually do a bit to improve her father's situation.

"That's perfect with me," Nadine quipped. "I can't seem to get any work done today, so anytime he can make it is fine." She debated saying the next thing, then decided that she could confide further in Annie. "Just between you and me, this thing with Rutledge trying to make me back off really has me rattled—not to mention hopping mad," she added.

"And you're sure the people who are following you are working for the oil company that forced Uncle Al to sign over the fracking rights?" Annie asked.

"Who else would it be?" Nadine wanted to know. "Dad's not exactly a lovable person, but the oil company is the only one with something to gain—and my digging into their actions is making them really uncomfortable—something else that tells me I'm right to suspect there's something shady going on."

"You know," Annie speculated, "I can't believe that Uncle Al would sign over his fracking rights voluntarily. He's such a stubborn man and no one could ever talk him into doing anything he didn't want to."

Nadine sighed before she caught herself. "You remember him the way he was, Annie," she told her cousin. "Dad's not quite like that anymore." There was a trace of mournfulness in her voice, a trace she would only allow to come through around her family.

"How bad is he?" Sympathy echoed in every one of Annie's words.

"Well, he's got more good days than bad," Nadine informed her, doing her best to hang on to that thought for as long as she could. "But sometimes," she admitted, "when I look at him, I can see that he's not really there at all. Oh, Annie, it's such an awful, awful disease, robbing everyone, not just the victim.

"Don't get me wrong," Nadine was quick to add. "Most days, Dad is his usual feisty old self and you couldn't tell that there was *anything* wrong—except for maybe his less-than-friendly disposition. And pride won't let him have anyone living at the house to help, not since Mom died. But he's always been like that," she reminded Annie. "He can be like that for probably weeks at a time. And then, suddenly, for no apparent reason, he'll just disappear into himself."

Her mouth suddenly went dry as the words she uttered weighed heavily on her tongue.

Taking a breath, she continued before Annie could make a comment—or worse, pity her. "Luckily," Nadine said, "it doesn't last all that long. It's kind of like his mind is playing hide-and-seek with his brain. But it's really very scary while it's going on."

"Well, I can't help with any of that," Annie admitted regretfully. "But at least I can have Caleb work on getting that oil company to back off. If he's successful, he might be able to get the oil company to give back fracking rights that go with it it."

Hope reared its head once again. She could almost feel it coursing through her veins.

"Do you really think that's possible?" Nadine asked. "I mean, I'm sure they tricked Dad, but is there any way to even prove that?"

"If anyone can find a way, Caleb can," Annie assured her.

Nadine paused for a moment. Normally, she

wouldn't ask her cousin this sort of personal question, but these were not normal times.

"If he's really that good, that conscientious, what made the two of you break up? I don't even remember what it was five years ago," Nadine asked. "I know it's none of my business, but I have to confess you've made me curious."

"Let's just say that we were better at being friends than being a couple," Annie said. "The problem with Caleb is that he has a great deal of integrity. Much more than his share."

There was no bitterness in her voice. It was just the way things were, Annie thought.

"He was always rushing off to somewhere because he was trying to make up for everything his father had done or to work with the Truth Foundation, as you might recall. Caleb insisted on carrying the entire burden on his shoulders, trying to deal with the shame and humiliation his father had caused his mother and the rest of the family. Not to mention that Caleb put *all* of his energy into trying to make up for what his father did while a judge on the bench, sentencing so many people to years in jail when they could have been given lighter sentences— or set free altogether.

"Are you still there, Nadine?"

"I'm still here. That sounds just awful," Nadine couldn't help telling her cousin. She felt bad for

Caleb, but at the same time, she admired the fact that he was trying to right wrongs that had been done   same as her.

"Oh, it was," Annie said. "And I'm just speaking from secondhand knowledge," she pointed out. "The amazing thing is that Caleb's mother never resented her husband for any of what it turned out he put her and the rest of the family through. She really stuck by the man.

"I have a feeling she would have stuck by him through his trial and any sentence that the judge gave him. Lucky for Ben Colton, though, he wound up not having to face any of it."

Nadine was familiar with the particulars of the tragedy. Everyone in the area was, even though it had taken place all those years ago. "I wouldn't exactly call dying in a freak auto accident 'lucky,'" she pointed out.

Annie disagreed. "Oh, I think that Caleb's father would have. He was a very proud man and, after all the heights he had risen to, plummeting down that far and then possibly being sent to the same prison he had sentenced others to might have actually amounted to absolute torture for him.

"This was actually the better way out—for Ben. And, eventually, for all of his victims. Caleb made sure that as many of the victims who were still alive all received restitution for what they had gone through. The money from his father's insurance policy was awarded to several victims' families."

"What about Caleb's mother?" Nadine asked. "Didn't she need the money?"

"The money was used with Isa Colton's blessing," Annie said. "Like I said, she is a very rare woman. Didn't I already tell you all this?"

"Some of it is beginning to come back to me," Nadine admitted. "But not the bulk of it. You know, Caleb's mother might have been a forgiving woman," she went on. "But me, I would have just wanted to go for the jugular over something like that. For instance, what that oil company executive—or henchman—did was absolutely awful, and as far as I'm concerned, the man—or woman—should be drawn and quartered for the way they took advantage of my father when his mind was so obviously on hiatus."

"Given Caleb's integrity, I'm sure he would agree with you. The first step, though," she reminded Nadine, "is proving it."

Nadine laughed softly as she thought that comment over. "That first step, though," she agreed, "is a real doozy."

"I don't doubt it, but trust me, if anyone can get to the bottom of all this and make the oil company back off, Caleb is your man. Just be honest with him and be sure to tell him everything," Annie counseled.

"I wasn't planning on doing anything else," Nadine told her. She was a great believer in honesty.

"Good. Let me know how it goes."

"I'll be sure to give you a firsthand report," she promised her cousin.

"I'll be waiting," Annie said. "Talk soon," she said just before she terminated the call.

Nadine hung up the receiver and then pushed the landline farther back on her makeshift desk. There was nothing she could do at the moment except wait.

And maybe cross her fingers, she thought.

She didn't do waiting very well. She was more of a take-charge type of woman when it came to getting justice. Was Caleb the same way?

Nadine's eyes strayed toward the unfinished earrings she had pushed aside earlier. Since she was supposed to be sitting and waiting, she told herself that she could at least be productive and earn some money while she was doing this sitting. Heaven knew that money would certainly come in handy right about now, she thought. She sincerely doubted that ex-in-law or no, Caleb Colton would not offer his services cheap.

With that in mind, Nadine forced herself to focus on creating the best pair of earrings that she was capable of creating. She had been a jewelry maker for a number of years now and liked the freedom of being her own boss.

Nadine sat down and went to work.

* * *

It took some doing, but Caleb finally managed to get back to the office at ten minutes to six. It was who he was.

No matter what other people did, Caleb had always hated being late for anything—big or small. That was what had caused him to always be on time from an early age. He had practically made being on time—or more accurately, being early—into a religion.

As he entered the suite of offices, Caleb passed the assistant that he shared with his twin sister. As he walked by, he glanced in Morgan's direction.

When their eyes met, Rebekah Hanlan shook her head.

"She's not here yet," the older, tastefully dressed assistant informed him.

"Let me know the minute she gets in," Caleb told the woman.

Rebekah looked at him as if he had started babbling nonsense. She had known Caleb and his twin ever since they had to take over the law firm.

"I wasn't planning on holding her captive," she cracked.

It had been one of those long, endless days that just insisted on going go on and on, but somehow, the sarcastic remark did the trick. The comment managed to infuse enough of a spark within him to bring some life back into his veins.

"Good to know, Rebekah." He nodded down the hall. "I'll be in my office."

"And here I thought I'd have to send out a search party to find you," Rebekah quipped. "I'll send this Nadine person in when she arrives—provided she does arrive."

"According to my ex-wife, the woman is more than desperate. She'll arrive," Caleb assured her with confidence.

"Uh-huh," Rebekah murmured, sounding less than convinced regarding what he had just expressed.

Caleb didn't have time to debate Rebekah. He just wanted to meet with Nadine, get a few things squared away and, heaven willing, go home to get a little dinner and down a well-deserved nightcap.

He'd reached out to a PI he worked with and ordered a full background check run on her. The woman was definitely someone who couldn't be labeled *boring* in any sense of the word, Caleb thought. From the looks of things, when she took on a cause— and she had taken on more than her share—she didn't do so in half measures. Instead, Nadine apparently threw herself headlong into everything that she undertook.

Compared to Nadine, Caleb couldn't help thinking, Annie was laid-back. Nadine didn't seem to hold back at all.

Ever.

Well, he thought, it took all kinds. He just hoped that this crusader wouldn't bug him too much. They both seemed to seek out justice for others, but in different manners. From the bits and pieces he had put together, it seemed that Nadine Sutherland had a knack of rubbing people the wrong way. And although it was always for a good cause, he was in no mood for putting up with that, Caleb thought.

"Oh, the things we do for family," he muttered to himself.

The next moment, it struck him that, despite the fact that they were no longer married and that Annie had gone on to marry someone else and create a family with that man, he still thought of the Sutherlands as his kin. Maybe not first tier, the way he thought of his mother and his siblings, but Annie was most definitely family, he thought with an ironic smile.

Just then, Caleb heard the computer on his desk buzz, rousing him out of his thoughts. That was Rebekah's way of getting in contact with him from her desk.

"Yes, Rebekah?"

"She's here," Rebekah announced, not bothering to say the woman's name. "Do you want me to send her in?"

"Can't talk to her while she's out there and I'm in here, now, can I?" he asked the assistant matter-of-factly.

"Just thought you'd want a couple of minutes to pull your thoughts together," Rebekah informed him crisply.

He knew the assistant was fishing for some sort of a compliment or acknowledgment of her efficiency. There was nothing to be gained by not doing so.

"That's very thoughtful of you, Rebekah, but my thoughts are as pulled together as they're going to be. You can send her in."

"Will do," Rebekah answered. Then Rebekah brought Annie's cousin into his office.

Chapter 4

Because politeness had been instilled in him from a very young age, Caleb slowly rose in his chair when Nadine was brought into his office.

Even though he had seen a great many photos taken of her, he couldn't take his eyes off the woman in front of him.

Nadine Sutherland looked to be about five-seven, had a very slim, athletic build and dark brown, shoulder-length hair that was shot through with auburn highlights. She couldn't have been described as drop-dead gorgeous, but she had the kind of face that lingered on a man's mind long after the impression created by a stunner would have just faded away.

It was hard to reconcile that face with the woman who had a string of arrests attached to her, even if all those arrests were attributed to nonviolent marches for a whole list of causes that she espoused and was devoted to.

Caleb put his hand out in greeting. "Nadine?" he asked by way of creating an actual connection between them.

"That's what my dad calls me," she answered, secretly wondering just how much longer that particular piece of information would continue to be true. Anticipating the day her father no longer recognized her filled her with sorrow.

The next moment, she found herself thinking that Annie's ex looked more like a handsome male model in a high-end fashion magazine than a lawyer.

"Why? Were you expecting someone else?" she suddenly asked, thinking that something might have come up since Annie had spoken to him earlier today and he was scheduled to meet another person at this time. "Because if you are, I can come back tomorrow morning—or wait, or—"

"No, no 'or,'" Caleb told the woman, stopping her from continuing and waving a hand at her protests. "Why don't you just take a seat and we'll talk about why you're here."

Rebekah, who had brought the woman in, did not

appear to be leaving. "Thank you, Rebekah," he said formally. "You may go home now."

Rebekah's eyes swept over Nadine, then went back to Caleb. "Are you sure about that? Because I can stay if you need me."

"I won't be needing you," he informed her with finality, then, glancing at Nadine, he promised, "This won't take long." His attention went back to Rebekah. "I'll see you tomorrow."

The assistant shrugged her shoulders. "Have it your way," she murmured, then walked out of the office.

When he looked back at Nadine, he saw Nadine staring at him. "Sounds like you've decided that this is over before it's even started."

"Not exactly," Caleb felt honor bound to state. It was, he immediately realized, an unfortunate choice of words on his part.

"Then, *what* 'exactly'?" Nadine wanted to know.

He had to tell her what was on his mind after having done his investigation into who this woman was. "I have to admit that I do have my doubts about whether someone is harassing you," Caleb admitted.

"Go on," Nadine told him.

There was an edge in her voice. The kind of edge that let Caleb know the woman he was talking to was preparing herself for a less-than-friendly confrontation.

Caleb pushed on. Saying anything less than the truth seemed disingenuous to him. He had always been a great believer in honesty.

"In an effort to make sure that I would render you the best possible help that I could, I had a background check run on you today," he told her.

Nadine stared at him. Annie hadn't said her ex was such a stick-in-the-mud. His action only meant one thing to her   that he viewed her to be some sort of an emotional troublemaker.

She raised her chin. He wouldn't be the first, she thought in annoyance. There were members of her own family who thought of her that way. That had never stopped her from doing what she felt was right.

"You have a great many arrests on your record," Caleb continued.

She had told herself that since this was Annie's ex and he was supposedly doing her a favor, she would hear him out. But the moment he said anything about her arrests without even mentioning the causes she had undertaken instantly put her back up. Logically, she knew he wouldn't have been able to come to any other conclusion if he had run that background check on her, but she wasn't looking for logical. She was looking for empathy, for understanding—and he wasn't displaying any of that. But did he even know about her dad's condition and what had been done to him?

Nadine took the only option open to her. She went on the attack. "Yes, I *do* have a lot of arrests next to my name," she agreed, "but that doesn't give you a reason to feel so smug and superior about the situation. Have you ever felt as adamant about anything the way I feel about the causes that I've undertaken and continue to undertake? Even with your foundation?"

Caleb's eyes narrowed. He wasn't about to give her a summation of all the causes and people he'd helped. "Forget about it."

He was bluffing, she thought. In striking out, she had managed to hit a nerve. "Why? Did someone try to ace you out of a parking space you had your eye on?"

The woman did have a way about her that could rub a saint the wrong way, he thought. *Really* rub them the wrong way.

But even so, there was something in her voice that managed to connect with him as well as *to* him.

Caleb answered, "As a matter of fact, I *have* felt adamant about something. Really adamant," he underscored. "In his capacity as a judge, my father wrongfully sent a lot of people to privately run prisons. He did that in exchange for money and for kickbacks.

"My twin sister and I started the Truth Foundation as a way to try to pay those people—in some cases, their families—back. In essence to try to make up for the suffering they had gone through because of my father."

"I thought you were a lawyer," Nadine said, thinking of the reason why she had agreed to have her cousin's ex-husband look into the matter for her. She needed a lawyer, not a saint trying to earn his halo.

"I *am* a lawyer," he answered. "But there's nothing in the rules that says I can't do good, too," Caleb pointed out. "The way I look at it, trying to make up for what my father did only helps me to increase the scope of my focus whenever I undertake any case."

Caleb had to admit that the list of Nadine's arrests had thrown him for a moment. Until she had gotten so defensive just now, he had forgotten the kind of feelings he had experienced trying to fix all those wrongs that his father had done.

There was no "good" reason for doing something so heinous just to be able to take care of his family.

He knew without asking that his mother and his siblings would have *all* been a great deal happier on far less if Ben Colton acted differently.

But there was no point in wishing for events of the past to be transformed. All he could do was move on and try to make amends as best he could.

That was all, he thought philosophically, that any of them could do.

"I'm not judging you," he told Nadine in an attempt to forestall any rift that might be in the making. He wanted her to understand that he was on her side. Admittedly, he had temporarily lost sight of that, but luckily, his "vision" had returned. "As a matter of fact, I applaud your dedication. Not everyone stands up for what they believe in or makes the kind of sacrifices that having a set of beliefs that aren't always popular requires."

She found herself waiting for the punch line, the words that would negate what he had just said. When it didn't come, she heard herself putting her skepticism into words.

"You're kidding, right?"

The woman was really defensive, Caleb thought. He found himself feeling sorry for her and whatever had made her react this way.

Thinking back to what Annie had said about her cousin and the things he had gleaned from what he had read, Caleb realized this was what happened when a person found themselves fighting battles all on their own. Caleb had no doubt that there were lots of "warriors" out there who had taken part in the protests. But in the end, Nadine evidently fought these battles by herself.

Thinking fast, Caleb decided that it was time for Nadine not to feel as if she was waging a war on her own.

"Has any fracking started on your father's property yet?" he inquired.

"No, but it's scheduled to start by the end of the month," Nadine answered. The frown on her face seemed to travel clear down to the bone.

Caleb nodded. "Good."

"Good?" she questioned, stunned. "How could something like that be thought of as 'good'?"

"Because if it hasn't started yet, this is the best time to get a stay in place against the fracking that's *about* to begin on your dad's property."

"Really?" she questioned. "You can actually get a stay put in place?"

For the first time since she had found out about this awful development involving her father's so-called "deal" with the oil company, a deal he professed to have no memory of and refused to discuss, she felt real hope.

Maybe she was just being premature and foolishly optimistic, Nadine thought, but she clung to that hope, absorbing it and taking refuge in that positive feeling.

Caleb nodded his head to confirm what he had just told her. Embarrassingly, his stomach chose that exact moment to rumble and remind him that he had been so busy with one thing and another today, his last meal of memory had been breakfast.

His stomach rumbled again, a bit more insistently

this time. "As you've probably guessed, I haven't had anything to eat since early this morning."

Nadine felt her optimistic feeling fading away. She knew this had been too good to be true, she thought. He was using his rumbling stomach as a way to retreat and get out of resolving her father's situation.

"I didn't mean to keep you from your dinner," Nadine began, resigning herself to giving the man a way out.

Caleb looked at Annie's cousin, his mind racing as he made a quick calculation. He really didn't just want to leave her up in the air about this situation.

"Listen, why don't you come with me to dinner?" Caleb suggested. "We can eat and discuss the possible next steps that are available to you and that you can take in order to fight whatever fracking claim Rutledge Oil thinks it can get away with. What do you say?"

Nadine paused and thought for a moment. Usually, when someone was trying to hit on her, all sorts of radar would go off in her head. Most men, she had come to realize, didn't see past her looks. Over time, it had made her more than a little suspicious.

But she had a feeling this wasn't about the attorney possibly hitting on her. Annie's ex was being sincere, not to mention genuine. Despite her initial wariness, Nadine had a feeling that Caleb meant what he said about not just wanting to help her but intended to come up with a way to put that "help" into real action.

Besides, he was talking about going out to eat. That meant out in public at a restaurant. It wasn't as if he was planning on whisking her off to his apartment or some hotel room.

And even if that *was* his intention, Nadine thought, she was a big girl. A big girl who knew how to take care of herself.

She needed to stop having her imagination run away with her.

"All right," Nadine agreed. And then she asked, "What restaurant are we going to?"

He saw that she had taken her cell phone out of her purse. Caleb raised a quizzical brow as he looked at her phone. "Atria. Why, are you going to call and make a reservation?" he wanted to know, somewhat amused. "If that's what you're thinking," he said, giving her a way out, "there's no need. I have a long-standing friendship with the owner."

"I'm calling Annie."

She had lost him again. He didn't understand. "Why?"

Nadine grasped at the first thought that occurred to her. "I told Annie I'd let her know how everything went."

"It hasn't 'went' yet," Caleb pointed out good-naturedly. "It's ongoing."

Even as Caleb said that, he couldn't help wondering if Nadine was calling her cousin because she wanted Annie to know where she was going to be.

But then, thinking back again on the background check, he supposed that he couldn't really blame her. All the people—and their families—that his father had duped when he had been on the bench must have felt the same thing about him.

"Tell Annie I said hi," he told Nadine as he rose from his chair and crossed over to where he had hung up his overcoat.

Their eyes met for a moment. He looked confident and completely unfazed that she was calling the person who had asked him for this favor.

This man, Nadine decided, was on the level. The last fragments of her distrust totally slipped away.

She closed her phone again.

"Can't get a signal?" Caleb guessed, putting on his overcoat.

He had brought hers over, as well, and now went to help her on with it. He was careful not to allow his hands to linger on her shoulders, although Caleb had to admit it was difficult not to. Despite his reservations, he was finding himself intrigued by Nadine Sutherland and her passionate nature, as well as attracted to her.

"I've decided to call her later, after we've had dinner and talked."

"Does that mean you've decided to trust me?"

he asked, crossing to the office door and holding it open for her.

She started to protest that he didn't need to hold the door for her, then decided she was being too defensive. "I've decided to go with my gut instinct," she said to Caleb, walking out. "Besides, I've never been to Atria. Eating there might be fun."

"Well, it's definitely tasty," Caleb assured her.

"Why don't we go in my car?" he suggested once they were outside the building. "After we've had dinner, I'll drive you back here, but there's no reason for both of us to drive to the restaurant separately."

She supposed that did make sense, and now that she had relaxed a little, at least enough to trust the man, there was no point in both of them looking for parking spaces.

"Okay," Nadine agreed, surprising him as they approached his vehicle. "I agree."

Chapter 5

"So, is Atria the way you envisioned it would be?" Caleb asked Nadine after they had been shown to a table that was off to the side of the restaurant and the receptionist had handed them each their menus.

"I'm not sure what I was expecting," Nadine answered, looking around after Caleb had helped her with her chair. "But it's very homey." The restaurant's lighting struck her as just right. Not too bright and not too dim. "Is the food as good as they say?" she asked him.

"Better," he replied confidently. "Why don't you open your menu and see if there's anything that looks particularly good to you," Caleb suggested, "and you can find out for yourself."

Nadine left the menu closed in front of her. "To be honest, I lost my appetite the day I found out about what Rutledge Oil had done."

"Righteous anger is all well and good," Caleb told her. "But we can't have you passing out from hunger at what could turn into an inopportune moment."

His wording amused her despite herself. "Is there an 'opportune' moment to pass out from hunger?" Nadine asked.

"When you're trying to rouse empathy or a sense of kinship from a third party," he said without any hesitation.

Nadine smiled at the attorney. He seemed to have a sense of humor, but he was also serious about taking on her fight, she thought. That made her feel hopeful.

"I'll keep that in mind," she said, referring to what he'd just said about arousing sympathy.

Caleb caught himself thinking that Nadine had a very captivating smile. It wasn't the kind of smile that caused all sorts of unbidden thoughts to suddenly rise up in a man's mind, crowding to the forefront. It was a genuine, compelling smile that instantly made someone want to befriend this woman.

In his opinion, it must be her best weapon when she marched for all those causes she espoused. As a matter of fact, in some cases, one look at that smile of hers could make someone instantly change sides, Caleb mused.

Unless, of course, the people in range of that smile were underhanded, soulless henchmen who were determined to steal what they couldn't buy outright.

He felt himself growing indignant and immediately put a lid on his reaction. This was about dinner, not the oil company, and he didn't want to jump to conclusions. He intended to look into the company and their dealings at length. But first things first.

"But for now," Nadine went on to say, "I think I'll go on remaining upright."

"Okay, then you'll eat," he concluded, his tone indicating that her choice at the moment was a simple cut-and-dried one.

Nadine wanted things between them to remain clear. "There's no need to buy me dinner," she told the attorney.

"No one said anything about 'need,'" Caleb stated matter-of-factly. "I just find it awkward to eat in front of someone who is stoically abstaining from having any food." He leaned in a little closer. "When did you last eat?" he asked unexpectedly.

She raised her eyes to his. "Do you want the truth or do you want me to make something up?"

This was an unusual conversation for her and she was trying to buy some time. Ordinarily, she would have just created a convenient fiction that suited her needs. But there was nothing ordinary about this conversation. Or, she was beginning to think, the man she was having it with.

"The truth," Caleb instantly responded. "Always the truth."

The way he had just said it, Nadine felt that he actually strongly believed in that credo. How about that! She had actually found an honest man, she thought.

"Sometime this morning," she admitted vaguely.

Since there had been nothing outstanding about the meal to set it apart from any other meal she'd had in recent memory, the event had just melded into all the other meals that she'd had of late, usually on the run.

"Then you'll have something to eat." Caleb said the words as if they were a foregone conclusion.

It wasn't that she didn't want to eat; it was just that she really didn't want to waste any time doing it. If the man was pressed for time, Nadine didn't want to waste any of that time eating. She wanted to spend it talking and planning.

But he was the one laying down the terms, she reminded herself. His beach, his ocean, so she might as well just agree and save them all a lot of time.

Flipping open the menu, she glanced down the columns and made her decision.

"I'll have the shrimp scampi," Nadine said, closing her menu and setting it down on the side of the table.

"And?" Caleb prodded, his eyes meeting hers.

Was he talking about something to drink, she wondered. Alcohol, taken in the proper amounts, didn't make her fuzzy, but she had taught herself to abstain from it unless she was in the company of someone she actually knew—*and* as long as it was a social occasion and not one that required any serious thought or discussion on her part. Consequently, she usually didn't partake these days. She wanted to remain sharp and understand everything that was said.

"Water," Nadine said, finally answering his question.

"Nothing else?" he asked as their server approached their table. "You're sure?"

"I'm sure," Nadine told him.

Nodding, he turned toward the server, gave the woman Nadine's order and then placed his own, which turned out to be down-to-earth. He ordered a medium-rare, bone-in steak with mashed potatoes and green beans. He also asked for a glass of red wine.

He closed the menu and looked at Nadine as he surrendered it to the server. "Last chance to change your mind."

Nadine shook her head. "I'm good," she assured the attorney.

His mouth quirked in a quick, fleeting smile as his eyes swept over the woman sitting opposite him.

"Obviously," he agreed.

Nadine felt her heart flutter a little and quickly tamped down her reaction. The man was a little too attractive for his own good, she thought.

The server returned almost immediately with Caleb's glass of wine and Nadine's glass of bottled spring water. She also brought a basket of warm dinner rolls and set that on the table between them.

Flashing a smile at her customers, the young woman promised, "Your dinners will be ready soon," and then retreated.

"Would you like a roll?" Caleb asked, moving the basket toward Nadine.

She shook her head. "No, not right now, thank you."

"Well, as my stomach already embarrassingly informed you, I'm starving," Caleb told her. He took the top roll out of the basket. "Warm," he commented the moment he picked it up. "There's just nothing better than a warm dinner roll."

As if to prove it, Caleb took a bite out of the one in his hand.

He closed his eyes then, savoring that first bite

as if he had just tasted something that was nothing short of heavenly.

"There's no doubt about it. Atria's got the best bread in the state. There's garlic in it, so it might put a cramp in a person's social life for the day, but I guarantee that it's well worth it—most definitely if you've got nothing planned for the rest of your evening," he added with a wink.

Nadine couldn't help wondering if he was pushing the rolls, or subtly telling her that she had nothing to worry about from him romantically or otherwise this evening.

Either way, he had managed to sell her on the rolls.

She eyed the near-full basket, finally breaking down. "Maybe I will give them a try."

The smile on his face rose all the way up into his eyes.

"You won't regret it," Caleb promised. Picking out a likely candidate for Nadine, he held the roll up to her lips, offering it to her. "Go ahead," he coaxed. "Take a bite. Nothing will ever seem the same again," he guaranteed with a grin.

She looked at him, thinking that sounded like overkill. She couldn't help wondering if there was some sort of additive included in the roll.

"It's just a roll, right?" she asked him cautiously.

"No," he said. "It's heaven in dough form."

Since he was still holding the roll for her to sample, she put her hands around his and brought the roll to her lips. Her eyes remained on his, and as she took that first bite, she could have sworn she felt a warm shiver dance up and down through her entire body.

Nadine wasn't all that sure if it was because of the roll, or the man who was holding it out to her. All she knew was that she hadn't experienced this sort of an electric reaction in a long, long time.

"Good?" Caleb asked, watching her face.

"Good," she echoed with assertion. After a moment, she finished eating the piece in her mouth and took a deep breath. It was time to get back to the real reason she was here. "I don't want to be a killjoy, but "

"You'd like to get back to talking about your father's case," Caleb guessed.

She nodded her head. "Exactly."

In all honesty, Nadine felt that she had just experienced an extremely strong connection between herself and Caleb and, if she didn't feel as if her back was up against the wall, maybe she would even be inclined to explore that further.

But she felt as if she was running out of time and she really didn't want to waste any of it, especially since it seemed like it was slipping away from her at an increasing speed. Especially when it came to her father.

The server arrived and brought their dinners. Setting them down unobtrusively, the server slipped away.

"Do you really feel that you can get some sort of an injunction?" she questioned, desperate for some actual reassurance.

Caleb wanted her to understand what his thoughts were based on. "Now that I think about it, I did meet your father back when I was first married to Annie. It was just the one time, but I remember that he made an impression on me. He was outspoken and grounded in his beliefs. He certainly wasn't the kind of person who was given to vacillating. And I seriously doubt that he could be talked into doing anything that he didn't wholeheartedly believe in."

Nadine wasn't sure that she followed what he was telling her. "So what are you saying? That you think my father actually did sign those papers willingly?"

Caleb set his knife and fork down for a moment. This was a lot more important than his steak and his pinched stomach. Al Sutherland could have sold the rights and his activist daughter could be lying, trying to revoke his actions, but somehow he didn't think so. Nadine's actions were too obvious to be covert.

"No, from what you've told me and what I witnessed, he would have hung on to anything he felt was his, which means that someone found a way to either hoodwink your father, or just out-and-out take advantage of him and get his signature on that document by subterfuge, especially if he has a reduced mental capacity.

"Either way, I think Rutledge Oil disingenuously obtained those fracking rights from your father. I'm going to investigate and find a way to prove what happened. I'll even do it pro bono."

Picking up the knife and fork, he resumed eating. The food here was just too good to ignore for long, Caleb thought, biting into another piece.

Nadine could have thrown her arms around the man's neck and kissed him, but that might have started something else entirely, something she wasn't prepared to follow through on. So for the time being, she just put her hand on top of his and squeezed it.

"If you could do that, I would be in your debt forever," she told him.

Caleb looked as if he was about to shrug off the declaration as if it was just something she had uttered in the heat of the moment.

Undeterred, Nadine wanted him to understand exactly what she was telling him. "I mean it. This is something I intend to pay you back for, no matter how long it takes." She was that grateful to him.

Caleb laughed, nodding at the plate that was sitting in front of her. "Well, for openers, you could eat your dinner before it gets cold."

Nadine smiled as she looked at him. "Shrimp scampi is good hot or cold."

"You just can't help arguing, can you?" he asked. But it wasn't meant as a critical comment.

And Nadine didn't take it as such. "I guess being stubborn is just in my blood," she said dryly.

Caleb finished his meal. He had to admit that being full felt a great deal better than running on empty.

"Well, if we wind up going to court over this, and I'm pretty sure that we will, you're going to have to work on controlling that penchant you have for arguing. Seriously," he emphasized.

Nadine was about to say something about what he had just said when the melodic chime of her cell phone interrupted their conversation.

She held up her hand, stopping Caleb from continuing. "Excuse me, it's probably my client, wondering if I made any progress on those earrings."

Caleb took a sip of his wine, nodding as he thought her words over. "Annie said something about that. That you like to design original pieces of jewelry."

Nadine shrugged as if it was no big deal. "It pays the bills," she replied.

Rummaging in her purse, she found her cell phone and took it out. Whoever was on the other end of the call hadn't hung up. She said, "This is Nadine Sutherland."

She fully expected to hear a woman's voice on the other end. Instead, what she heard was a metallic sound. The kind that was used when the person who was calling was attempting to disguise their voice.

This wasn't the first time she was hearing that, either.

The moment that eerie squawk came through the speaker, she stiffened and braced herself.

Sitting across from her, Caleb saw the change in Nadine's demeanor immediately. Her face had instantly paled, taking on the unnerving color of parchment.

Rather than say anything out loud, Caleb waved his hand in front of her to get Nadine's attention, then mouthed, "Who?"

She didn't respond. Instead, she had pressed her lips together, looking, he thought, not afraid but like someone who was bracing herself for something terrible to happen.

Whoever was on the other end of the call was definitely intimidating her. Caleb would bet money on it.

Chapter 6

Caleb quickly took out his cell phone and hit the first key. Someone responded on the other end immediately.

"Yes, boss?"

Caleb kept his voice low so that Nadine's caller couldn't overhear. "Jason, I want you to trace this call," he ordered, and then he gave the investigator Nadine's cell phone number.

Caleb looked in Nadine's direction, and using hand gestures, he indicated that she put her call on speaker and place the phone on the table between them. When she complied, he placed his own device close enough to be able to record.

Caleb couldn't help noticing that Nadine's hands were shaking, but he stifled the urge to take her hand in his in an effort to comfort her and show his support. Getting this recording was the important thing at the moment.

Fortunately, Caleb had several investigators who did work, like Nadine's background check, for him, Morgan and the Truth Foundation. Discovery of his father's deception had taught him not to take anything at face value.

The moment he'd set down his phone near Nadine's, the eerie voice crackled as he issued a threat to her.

"You were warned to stop sticking your nose where it doesn't belong. Now you're going to have to face the consequences for doing that."

And then the line went dead.

Picking up his own phone, Caleb immediately asked his investigator, "Did you manage to get a location?"

"Just a general area," Jason responded. "Whoever it was wasn't on long enough for me to pinpoint the exact location that the call was coming from." He did not sound happy about what he had just said.

It wasn't what he wanted to hear, but he was prepared for it. "Do the best you can," Caleb told his investigator. "I'll be in touch."

Closing the cell phone, he tucked it back into his

pocket as he looked at Nadine. Her face still looked extremely pale. "Are you all right?" he wanted to know.

Ordinarily, she would bluff her way through this, saying it would take more than a disembodied voice making threats to get to her. But the incident was still too fresh in her mind for her to shrug off. And besides, it was not the first time.

But the caller had threatened her with retaliation. That was a new development. Usually, he just ordered her to back off or she would regret it. He had gone past that now, telling her she was going to pay for what she had done. The implication made clear as to just how that payment was going to be extracted.

Caleb was still looking at her, waiting for an answer.

Nadine cleared her throat. "I've been better," she told him in a voice that was still somewhat shaky, even though she was desperately trying to hide that. Shifting the focus off herself, she asked, "Who did you call?"

"Jason D'Angelo, one of the investigators our law office has on retainer. I knew it was a long shot, but I was hoping he could trace the call."

"But he couldn't?" It was only half a question. The way things were going lately, this latest wrinkle didn't really surprise her.

"He's still working on it," Caleb answered, thinking that leaving his statement with a small opening for success allowed a drop of hope to dribble through for Nadine. He studied her face. "I take it this wasn't the first of those you've received."

"No." The way she said it left no room for any doubt that the warnings had had a definite edge to them.

Again, he struggled with the urge to comfort her, but Caleb pushed on. "The next logical question would be how many of those calls have you received?"

Nadine didn't have to stop to think about her answer. Each call, including this one, was indelibly etched in her mind.

"Three," she told him. And each call had left her feeling more vulnerable. "Mr. Deep Voice has called me three times. But this is the first time he said I was going to have to pay for 'ruffling' the oil company's feathers. Chickens have feathers, right?" It was a rhetorical question. He noticed that her voice was growing stronger. Any lingering fear was beginning to abate. "Seems rather appropriate, if you ask me."

Studying her, he thought he knew where her head was at. "It's good that you're not shaking in your shoes, but there's such a thing as being too brave," Caleb pointed out.

She raised her chin. She didn't like being told

how to act "I've been dealing with bullies for most of my life."

"I didn't say to let them scare you off. I just don't want you thumbing your nose at them, either." He thought back to the call she had just received. "If I don't miss my guess, it sounded like the person on the other end was a guy."

Her eyes narrowed as she grew more defensive. "So?"

"So," Caleb continued his thought, "I really doubt that the oil company picked him for his fetching demeanor."

"What's that supposed to mean?" she asked.

"It means," Caleb told her, "that he can probably hurt you."

"Well, I know a few things about taking care of myself—" she began to protest indignantly.

"I'm glad to hear that, but this isn't up for debate. You asked Annie and she asked me to help you. I intend to assist, which means that you're going to listen to what I have to say—and, like it or not, you're going to go along with it."

"Look—" Nadine began to protest. Taking on a fighting form had always helped her deal with any fear that might be building up within her. It made her feel more in control of the situation—and she needed that right now.

Caleb had raised his hand to get their server's attention. "We'd like the check, please," Caleb said to her once she approached.

Caleb waited until the young woman had left the immediate area before he said to Nadine, "I'm going to take you to your home."

Her brow furrowed. Had he forgotten? "But I left my car at your office," Nadine politely reminded him. "You said you'd take me back there so I could pick it up, remember?"

"I remember," he assured her. "But that was before I saw you get that phone call and overheard that creep threatening you. Don't worry. I'll have one of my investigators drive your car over to your place. Right now, my first priority is making sure that you're safe."

"I can be safe driving myself home," Nadine protested.

She refused to be thought of as some damsel in distress who was in need of rescuing. If she began thinking of herself that way, everything would just wind up collapsing on her.

"I'm not doubting you," Caleb emphasized. "My concern is about the people you're dealing with From what I picked up, they've just escalated the stakes in this little game they're bent on playing."

As he watched, Nadine straightened her shoulders. For all the world, she reminded him of someone who was bracing herself for a fight.

With him.

"But—" she began again, determined to state her protest to this man, in no uncertain terms this time.

But just then, the server returned, so Nadine held her piece. The young woman placed the check next to Caleb on the table.

He glanced at it, noting the amount as he opened up his wallet. Placing two fifties on the small tray, he added an extra twenty to cover a generous separate tip for the server.

Rising, he moved around behind Nadine and drew her chair out for her.

"Nadine, this matter is not up for discussion," he informed her in no uncertain terms, his voice polite but firm.

How did she get him to understand? She really didn't want to fight with someone who was supposed to be helping her.

"Look, you have impeccable manners, Caleb, but I wasn't discussing this with you, I was saying no," she informed him.

But Caleb shook his head. "Sorry, I'm afraid I can't hear you. It's just too noisy in here." With that, he escorted her out of the restaurant.

Forced to follow him to his car, Nadine got into his vehicle and buckled up. But he noticed her body language as he got in on the driver's side. Her arms were crossed defiantly in front of her chest.

"Is that your way of protesting my decision?" he wanted to know, starting up the vehicle.

"No," she said genially. "This is my way of not telling you my address so you're going to have to drive me back to your office and let me get my car."

"Sorry to disappoint you," Caleb told her, his tone matching hers as he pulled out of the parking lot, "but I already know where you live." She looked at him, surprise and disappointment mingling in her features. "I did a background check on you today," he reminded her.

"You're a brave woman, Nadine. No one is questioning that. But bravery doesn't have to include being foolhardy. As a matter of fact, to my way of thinking, bravery would definitely *exclude* being foolhardy or reckless. Do you agree?" he asked.

Nadine frowned, but she knew she couldn't argue with him. Much as she hated to admit it, he was making sense.

"I agree," she said grudgingly.

Caleb nodded. "That's much better." He glanced at the silent radio. "Want to listen to something?" he offered, about to turn it on.

"I take it you're all talked out?" Nadine guessed.

Caleb laughed at the suggestion. "I'm an attorney. I'm never 'all talked out,'" he told her.

"Fair enough." She nodded. "But I'd rather talk than listen to anything on the radio."

When she said that, she felt that she'd given Caleb an opening and expected him to start talking. When he remained silent, she glanced at him quizzically. There was a very thoughtful expression on his face.

What was that all about?

"That was your cue to start telling me how you think we can stop these people from doing what they appear to have their hearts set on doing." When Caleb still made no immediate acknowledgment, she shifted in her seat to look at him. "Caleb, did you hear what I just said?"

"I think you were right," he said thoughtfully, sounding preoccupied.

She had no idea what he was talking about or what he was referring to. "In English, please."

He glanced up into his rearview mirror again. A silver sedan he'd glimpsed a few minutes ago was still there, following them—not too close, not too far. He supposed that it could just be a coincidence.

There was only one way to test his theory, he decided.

Caleb turned right at the next corner.

The sedan turned right as well.

"You said you thought you were being followed," he told Nadine.

"I was," Nadine answered. "At least I thought I was," she amended.

It was easy with everything that was going on lately to allow her imagination to get carried away.

"You were right. You *were* being followed," Caleb added with finality, turning again at the very next intersection. This time he deliberately turned left.

The silver car turned left, as well, keeping up the same speed.

"You still might be," he underscored.

Nadine's breath caught in her throat as she twisted around in order to get a better look behind her. She had moved so fast, it felt as if the belt was cutting into her throat. Slipping her thumb beneath it, she moved it aside.

She didn't like what she saw. "It's the same car from yesterday."

There were a lot of silver sedans in the area, he thought. That was an exceedingly popular color for a car.

"Are you sure?"

Nadine had to remind herself to breathe. Somehow, this situation didn't feel as bad, because he was with her. Why, she didn't know.

"I'm sure. There's a slight crack in the front windshield on the right-hand side," she told Caleb with certainty.

He squinted as he looked up into the rearview mirror. She was right, he realized. "You can see that from here?" Caleb questioned. "You must have amazing vision."

"No," she denied. "Just a good memory. I threw a rock at the driver the first time I saw him following me. It was in an effort to make that Neanderthal realize that I wasn't going to be intimidated. I was also hoping that it would make him back off." She frowned to herself as the memory of the encounter came back to her. With a sigh, she told Caleb, "It didn't."

"You do realize that you can't keep taking those kinds of chances with these people, don't you?" he stated.

"Well, I wasn't about to lie down and play dead, either," Nadine said stubbornly.

"I'm more worried about one of the company's henchmen losing their temper and *making* you dead," Caleb informed her. From where he stood, that was entirely possible.

Nadine couldn't help laughing softly. It helped relieve some of the tension she was feeling right now. "You do know that's not grammatically correct, right?"

"I'm not interested in being grammatically correct," he said, stepping on the gas and putting distance between them and the driver who was following them. "I'm interested in keeping you alive."

He almost sounded as if he meant it, Nadine

thought. "That's very nice, Caleb," she responded, "but—"

"There is no 'but' here," he informed her sharply. "There's only the bottom line, you remaining alive."

Caleb was searching his rearview mirror again, looking for any sign that the silver sedan was keeping up with them. He thought he caught a glimpse of the vehicle and sped up again. He continued making unexpected twists and turns down the various streets until he was finally satisfied that he had lost the vehicle.

Caleb slowed his car down and Nadine looked around the immediate area, attempting to orient herself. She had thought she was fairly familiar with where she lived, but she had to admit that, at least for the moment, she felt completely lost.

Chapter 7

"Are we lost?" Nadine asked point-blank.

Despite the situation, Caleb had to admit that he liked the way Nadine had said "we" instead of "you" when she asked the question. Someone else would have been quick to point a finger at him for losing their way, since he was the one who was driving, but she had deliberately included herself in the mix.

Caleb slowly scanned the immediate area behind his vehicle, not just in his rearview mirror but also over both shoulders.

Their tail seemed to have disappeared.

"The important thing is that we've lost the car that was following us," he told his passenger. "But no, we're not lost. I know where we are and I can get us to your home from here." He glanced in her direction. "Better?"

"No," she answered honestly, "but getting there." She leaned back in her seat, doing her best to relax a little. It wasn't easy. "Where did you ever learn to drive like that?" she asked.

"One of the investigators who worked for our firm was an ex-secret service agent." A fond smile curved his mouth as he remembered working with the man. "When I learned that he had been in charge of training the other agents in evasive driving, I asked him to teach me."

That didn't make any sense to her. "You're an attorney, so why would you want to learn how to drive like that?"

"I thought that it might come in handy someday," he told her. "Obviously," he concluded, "it did."

Nadine sat up at attention the moment that the former warehouse that had been turned into a bunch of lofts came into view. "We're almost there," she announced with relief.

"I can see that," Caleb answered. She certainly didn't believe in conventional living quarters, he thought. He spared Nadine a glance. "I think this would be a good time to tell you that there's been a slight change in plans."

The wary look was back in her eyes as she turned them in Caleb's direction. "What kind of change?"

"I'm going to be sleeping on your sofa. If that doesn't work for you, throw a couple of blankets on the floor and that'll do," he said as he drew closer to the converted warehouse's underground parking.

"Why?" she questioned.

"Well, I find that blankets make a hard floor a lot easier to endure."

He knew what she meant, Nadine thought irritably. "I wasn't asking you why you wanted a blanket on the floor. I'm asking you why you would be on my sofa."

"Protecting you," he answered simply. "I want to make sure that the person who was tailing us in that car isn't going to be making a sudden appearance in your loft or however you choose to refer to your living quarters."

So much for being able to relax and reclaim her life, Nadine thought. "It's a loft," she told him, then asked, "You really think that he might turn up here?"

"I think that we would both rather have you be safe than sorry." Threading his way in, he pulled up in the first available space he saw. "So, you didn't answer me. Do I get the sofa or the floor?"

Nadine unbuckled her seat belt, but for the time being, she remained seated. Her entire loft was one large living space, technically divided by curtains and strategically placed furniture.

"I've got what passes for a spare bedroom just off my studio," she volunteered.

He wanted to be as close to her door as possible. "The sofa will be better for my purposes," he told her, explaining, "I want to be close to the front door so I can hear the intruder if anyone has any ideas about breaking in."

Getting out of the vehicle, he quickly came over to her side.

As he opened her door for her, Nadine got the impression that he was on his guard for someone to suddenly jump out of the shadows.

He continued looking around as he quickly brought her into the converted warehouse and escorted her up.

The second she opened the elevator gates, he ushered her in and then closed the door behind them.

Habit had her locking it even though she had her doubts that would actually stop whoever had been pursuing her.

When she turned around, she saw that Caleb was going around, taking in all the windows, pulling the blinds closed to separate them from the rest of the outside world.

She felt really isolated, Nadine thought, looking around her living quarters.

"Is all that really necessary?" she asked Caleb as he pulled the last blinds closed.

"You tell me." He made one more pass around all four corners of the large space. Satisfied, he turned toward the woman whose safety he had undertaken to guard.

"Just how much of a pest did you make yourself to the oil company?" he queried, looking over his shoulder toward Nadine. "From the sound of that call you received in the restaurant, my guess is that they won't be inviting you to any of their Christmas parties anytime soon."

"I'd say that you've guessed correctly," she answered. "Maybe you could call that former secret service agent to come over," she suggested. "Have him look around." No offense intended to Caleb, but she would rather put her life into the hands of a professional, if it came to that.

"I would if I could," Caleb freely admitted. Satisfied that he had seen to all the windows and made sure that they were locked and secured, he came over to the sofa and sat down.

"But?" she asked, waiting for the other part of his sentence.

"Porter died in a plane crash a year ago. It was a tremendous loss to the team. He was a really good man," Caleb couldn't help adding. "Taught me a lot about being able to take care of myself as well as anyone else."

The revelation took her by surprise. "I'm sorry for your loss," she said with genuine sympathy.

"Thank you," he responded. He laughed softly to himself. It was funny how life arranged itself. "You know, losing Porter was harder on me than losing my father. Despite his previous career as a secret service agent, John Porter was exactly what he seemed. There were no deceptions, no pretenses."

His expression hardened a little. "Unlike my father," he told her. "Everyone thought that my father was such an upstanding, principled, charming man. Exactly the way you would envision a judge to be. I was really proud of being his son.

"It was a house of cards," he went on to admit. There was a bitter edge to his voice. "And when it came down, we were all judged to be as guilty as him."

He turned toward Nadine. "Porter was the one who helped me make peace with all that, made me see that my father's 'sins' had nothing to do with me or with anyone else in my family. The sins he was guilty of belonged to my father alone."

She got that, but she also knew what he and the others had been trying to do for the last ten years, thanks to Annie. "But that didn't stop you and your twin sister from trying to make up for what your father did to all those people and their families," she pointed out.

He laughed to himself, remembering everything that had transpired those last few years before the police came for the judge. "My father didn't exactly have a lock on justice—actual justice," Caleb emphasized. "The man wound up meting out a terrible form of 'justice' in order to build up that nest egg he was collecting in order to pay for the lifestyle he felt he needed to give to the family—and himself."

He suddenly paused and looked at Nadine, clearly bewildered. "How did we wind up on this topic?" he wanted to know. It wasn't in his nature to go on and on about himself, certainly not like this.

Nadine smiled. "I have a knack of drawing things out of people," she confessed. And then she laughed quietly. "I think it probably also comes from all that time I spent in holding cells, locked up with lot of other protestors who wound up getting arrested espousing the same causes I believed in and making their voices heard.

"When you're in there," she explained, vividly remembering, "waiting for a loved one—or not so loved one," she amended with a grin, "to post your bail, there's nothing much to do except either pace or talk. Since most of us had done a lot of pacing before we were incarcerated, that left talking."

She looked at Caleb, and for a second, he felt like he was the only one in the whole world besides her.

"You'd be surprised how little coaxing it took to get 'fellow protestors' to suddenly start making a clean break of things, telling me their deepest secrets, things they had no intention of saying just a few minutes ago."

Nadine smiled at him. "I guess that I've just got a face that people like to talk to."

Well, he certainly couldn't argue with that, he thought. Caleb realized that she had a very likable face. That had struck him while they were talking at the restaurant. And now that they were here in her studio loft, it seemed even more evident to him than ever.

"I guess you do," he commented.

For a second, she found herself tempted to draw closer. Catching herself, Nadine changed topics. "I just want you to know that I really appreciate you going out of your way like this," she told Caleb.

He smiled at her. Gratitude always made him feel a little uncomfortable, like he was out of his element.

"Don't mention it. It's just all part of the service."

She nodded her head and, making a decision, she rose to her feet. "Well, if you're going to be spending the night on my sofa, I'd better get you some bedding and some towels."

"Don't go to any trouble," he called after her. "Just a blanket will do."

"No, it won't," she called back, her voice echoing in the barnlike space. Returning in less than a couple of minutes, Nadine had her arms filled with sheets, a pillow, a blanket and several towels. "If I missed something," she told him, placing everything on the coffee table, "please let me know."

With that, she waved him off the sofa and then proceeded to make it up for him, covering the cushion with a bedsheet, then spreading another matching sheet over it so he could use that as well as the blanket on top of it to cover himself. Finished, Nadine placed a couple of pillows at one end.

"There. Done. I hope you find that comfortable. Like I said, if I left anything out, please let me know," Nadine urged her new protector.

"This looks great," he assured her. "Doesn't look like you left out anything. *And*, to be honest, I don't plan on doing all that much sleeping. Catnaps, maybe, but not out-and-out sleeping."

"Oh? Why?" Cocking her head, she waited for Caleb to continue explaining.

"I have to admit, I've never been a really heavy sleeper, not since—" He stopped himself abruptly. He was doing it again, he thought, and he didn't want to drag her any further into his family's trials and tribulations than he already had. "Well, 'since,'" he merely concluded.

"If I were a heavy sleeper," he told Nadine, veering off into another direction, "there wouldn't be much point in my being here 'guarding' you. Certainly not if I fell asleep on the job."

Nadine wavered. She hesitated to leave him like this. After all, when she came right down to it, the man was putting himself out for her, and twenty-four hours ago, he had only been vaguely aware of her existence. At that point, she had just been his ex-wife's cousin, nothing more.

"Can I get you anything else?" Nadine asked, at least wanting him to be entirely comfortable before she left him for the night.

"Well," he considered. "Instead of my wandering around at night, making noise, you can point me toward where the kitchen in case I get thirsty—and toward where the bathroom is, in case another need arises. After you do that, I'd like you to go to bed so at least one of us gets a good night's sleep—or what passes for a good night's sleep."

She nodded. Both requests sounded more than reasonable to her.

"That's the kitchen, on the far side of the living room. And the bathroom is that small alcove just down the hall, next to the linen closet. Is there anything else?" she asked.

He shook his head. "Can't think of anything," he told her. "I'll see you in the morning. What time do you get up?" he asked as the afterthought hit him. He assumed that she probably got up around eight, and he didn't want to be guilty of making any noise that might wake her up.

"Six."

That caught him off guard. "Why so early?" he asked.

"I thought I'd try to get some work in," she explained. "Lately, it feels like I've got what's akin to writer's block, except there's jewelry involved," she told him, the corners of her mouth curving in a self-mocking smile.

"Come again?"

"I make jewelry for a living," Nadine reminded him. "Someone tells me what they've envisioned, and I do my best to turn it into reality." She pointed to the other end of the loft. "My tools are over there. I draw the piece of jewelry in question, lay out the necessary pieces, and then when I'm satisfied with what I've envisioned, I forge it until it takes on the required shape." She knew she wasn't being very clear about how she went about the job of creation, but it was the best explanation she could give. What mattered most was that in the end, she always came through with the requested piece or pieces. She had yet to have an unsatisfied customer.

Caleb shook his head in pure wonder. "An activist and a jewelry maker. Quite a combination," he heard himself saying.

Nadine smiled at him. "I never cared very much for the ordinary," she confided.

"Obviously," he agreed. "Well, don't let my being here get in your way. You get started as early as you'd like. Most likely, I'll be up already. Now, good night," Caleb told her. There was finality in his voice this time.

Nadine took that as her cue to leave the immediate area and make her way to what passed as her sleeping quarters.

"Good night," she replied. "And thanks again."

"You're welcome again," Caleb responded good-naturedly.

Chapter 8

It didn't take long for Caleb to come to the conclusion that Nadine had to have purchased the most uncomfortable sofa he could ever remember lying on. As he sought to find at least a better position, he decided that what he was lying on was more like a torture rack than an actual couch.

Consequently, he wound up getting very little sleep, which actually turned out to be just the way he had wanted it.

Because of the sofa—and his mindset—he found himself waking up every fifteen minutes. Twenty, if he found he was particularly drowsy. It seemed like every noise caught his attention, but in reality, it seemed the way that the loft was constructed was responsible for the creaks and unusual groans that he could hear.

Still, Caleb remained alert, listening to each noise until it faded away and there was no reason to continue listening.

Around six thirty, he began to hear very distinct noises. Not from the loft, which seemed to be in the process of constantly settling, but from the kitchen sounds.

Sitting up against the back of the torture rack that Nadine had referred to as a sofa, Caleb turned toward the noises, wanting to verify that (a) he had actually heard what he thought he had heard and (b) that it wasn't actually someone attempting to break in.

Caleb was fairly certain that he saw a light coming from the far end of the loft. But it was dim, and in truth, it was difficult for him to actually make out anything.

Caleb rose from the sofa and tucked the small firearm he had brought with him into the back of the waistband of his pants. He had a permit to carry, and because of some of the people he had dealt with, he always carried it with him. Last night, he had taken the gun out and left it under the sofa cushion for quick access if he suddenly needed it.

Because of the close-to-sleepless night he had spent, Caleb was having difficulty acclimating his eyes to the darkness as he made his way toward the kitchen.

Halfway across the loft, he let out the breath he had been holding as he relaxed. "I assumed you were kidding, but it looks like you really do get up at six."

Startled, Nadine swung around, stifling the scream that had instantly risen in her throat. She had also dropped the cracked open egg she was about to fry. The egg landed on the floor, the yolk oozing out on the freshly cleaned tile. Swallowing a curse, Nadine grabbed a paper towel, determined to mop up as much of the mess as possible.

Armed with a handkerchief, Caleb evidently had had the same thought. The result was that their heads wound up meeting directly over the yellow pool on the floor, unceremoniously bumping against one another.

Nadine emitted another sharp cry as she tried not to fall backward after their heads hit.

Caleb managed to catch her by her arms, succeeding in steadying her. The egg and the mess that had been created were temporarily forgotten.

Nadine looked at Caleb, annoyed with him and with herself for her reaction. Her nerves were supposed to be steadier than that, she silently upbraided herself.

"Didn't anyone ever teach you not to sneak up on a person in the dark?" she accused, embarrassed.

"Sorry," he apologized. "I did start talking as soon as I realized that it was you."

Calming down, she told him, "Too little, too late." Gesturing toward the small table in the corner, she suggested, "Why don't you just sit down at the table while I finish making breakfast?"

Caleb looked at the remaining mess. "The least I can do is tidy the floor," he said.

"No," Nadine contradicted. "The least you can do is sit at the table. I'll clean up." A smile slipped over her lips as she added, "There's less of a chance of another collision that way." With that, Nadine pulled another paper towel off the roll and wiped away the rest of the yellow liquid.

He didn't like standing around inactive this way. "Is there *anything* I can do?" Caleb asked.

Nadine looked in his direction. "By my reckoning, you were up for most of the night. The way I see it, you've done everything you can do. I don't want you suddenly collapsing on the floor because you didn't get any sleep. This breakfast, by the way," she continued as she worked, "is my small way of thanking you for standing guard over me. No matter what I sound like, I really appreciate your gallantry."

"Couldn't very well go off and leave you, now, could I?" Caleb asked.

She tossed out the paper towels and washed her hands, then got back to making breakfast. "I suspect that someone else might have done just that," she told him.

"I'm not someone else," he answered.

She turned then and looked at him over her shoulder. "No, that you are not," she agreed. "You are uniquely you, and while we're at it, I want to thank you for taking me seriously. People usually don't—except for Annie," she amended. "Other people in the family usually think I'm either exaggerating things or imagining them—or just plain flaky."

"Well, you definitely weren't exaggerating that call you got in the restaurant. I heard it," he reminded her.

To be honest, he was surprised she hadn't freaked out, that she had stayed as together as she had after being on the receiving end of that call. In his opinion, a lot of other people would have gotten really frightened after hearing that unnerving, metallic voice threatening them.

Thinking of how she must have felt hearing that voice, Caleb felt a wave of sympathy washing over him. "Whoever is after you and your dad, we'll get them," he promised.

She smiled up at him. Caleb was a lot nicer than she had first thought he was. "Well, until you do, why don't we have breakfast?" she said.

Nadine placed both plates of bacon, eggs and toast down on the table. And then she stopped abruptly, raising her eyes to his face as a thought suddenly hit her. "You're not a vegan, are you?"

He met her question with a soft laugh. "Not even remotely. If I were a vegan, I'd have to give up all meat and I'm really not ready to do that," he told her with feeling. "Besides, I had a steak last night," he reminded her.

When had she gotten so scattered? "I'd forgotten about that," she admitted. "And I'm fresh out of cereal," she added, which would be her only other option, normally.

Turning away, Nadine made her way over to the coffee maker that had just finished percolating. She poured them each a cup, then she brought the coffees over and set the cups down next to the milk and sugar.

"Go ahead," she coaxed, nodding toward the plates. "The breakfast isn't going to eat itself."

"This is good," Caleb told her with sincerity after he'd had a chance to swallow that first mouthful.

Her mouth curved with amusement as she sat down over her own plate. "It's a little hard to ruin something as simple as fried eggs and bacon," Nadine pointed out.

A memory of some of his first breakfasts with Annie popped up in his head. Caleb laughed to himself. "You'd think so, wouldn't you? But you would be surprised how many people have managed to do that."

Nadine suspected that he was just trying to make her feel good, but she was not about to argue with him, not over something so minor. She had learned to save arguments for major confrontations, not minor conversations about eggs.

She finished her own quickly enough. "I can make you more if you're still hungry after you finish that," she volunteered, nodding at his plate.

"No, this is just enough." And then Caleb glanced at his watch just before he continued eating.

Nadine picked up on that. "You have to go somewhere after you finish eating, don't you?" she guessed.

He hadn't thought he was being that obvious. "Actually, I do," he admitted. He felt obligated to fill her in. "Arrangements were made before any of this came up," he told her, referring to his having come home with her last night.

Finished eating, he wiped his mouth, put the napkin on his plate and then turned his attention to the coffee.

Nadine noted that he took his coffee black. Unlike her. Her coffee was almost pale in comparison, and there was enough sugar in it to qualify the drink to fill in as a candy substitute.

"Well, by all means, go," she urged. "I wouldn't want to keep you," she told Caleb honestly.

But he shook his head. "I don't like the idea of leaving you alone," he explained to her, not after hearing about the type of person she could be dealing with.

His protest struck her as being extremely sweet, but she didn't want Caleb to feel obligated to hover over her. She felt braver now. Daylight had a way of doing that, and it was definitely getting lighter outside. Despite the drawn curtains, the growing illumination was nudging its way into the loft, making everything feel more positive.

"I was alone before I met you at your office," Nadine reminded him.

Caleb was only half listening to what she was saying. A thought suddenly hit him. Looking at her, he proposed, "Why don't you come with me?"

Nadine all but did a double take, then stared at him. The question had come completely out of the blue, and she really wasn't prepared for it. "Where?"

He realized he hadn't told her where he had to go. "To my mother's."

Nadine felt even more confused than she had a minute ago. Annie had mentioned how caught up her ex was with his family, but she had assumed that involved making amends to the people his father had wronged. She understood—she was still really close with her own dad.

"Excuse me?"

"I promised my mother I'd swing by her place today—before Annie called about you and your 'problem,'" he explained delicately. "I promise this isn't going to take long, and then I can focus my attention on you and whoever is threatening you at the oil company."

The idea of tagging along as he stopped by his mother's was not exactly something that warmed her heart. For one thing, Nadine didn't like butting in where she didn't belong.

"I'm sure your mother isn't going to be all that thrilled that you're bringing your ex-wife's cousin over, especially since I've been arrested and have a rather lengthy 'rap' sheet by some standards," she told him.

In her experience, although her heart was in the right place with every single cause she undertook, being arrested didn't exactly make her someone a man's mother would dream of having her son bring home.

Caleb hadn't expected that he would have to convince Nadine to come with him. "My mother is extremely open-minded." He could see that his words didn't convince her. "Look, if she never condemned my father for all the things he did, you being arrested for standing up for things you believed in is certainly not going to have her looking at you cross-eyed.

"Besides, you'll like my mother," Caleb promised, adding, "Everyone does."

She sighed. "Of course you'd have to say that," Nadine replied, pointing out the obvious. "You're her son."

"Be that as it may," he said, waving away her statement, "everyone likes my mother. I guarantee you, you will, too." He looked at her, waiting for her response. "What do you say?"

He'd been more than kind to her. And, she reminded herself, he was the first one besides Annie who had taken her seriously.

"I'd have to shower and get ready," she told him, thinking that he would probably tell her to never mind, because he had to leave now.

But he surprised her by saying, "Go ahead. I didn't give my mother any specific time that I'd be swinging by, I just said I'd be there in the morning."

Well, she'd painted herself into a corner, she thought.

"Okay," Nadine reluctantly agreed. She looked toward the sink. "But I have to wash the dishes first. I hate having things piled up," she said.

Caleb waved her away. "Go shower. I'll take care of the dishes," he replied. He saw the look of surprise on her face and grinned. "I know how to clean up after myself. My mom taught us."

Something wasn't making sense. "But didn't you grow up privileged? Or at least thinking you were privileged?" she asked.

"Didn't matter," he assured her. "My mother felt that, rich or not, we always needed to clean up after ourselves. Too bad that lesson was lost on my father," he commented.

Nadine looked back at the dishes doubtfully. She couldn't argue with him about this. It seemed silly. "Well, if you're sure."

Caleb shooed her toward the bathroom. "I'm sure," he told her.

"Okay."

Nadine went by the area she had fashioned into her bedroom and quickly picked up some fresh clothes. Armed, she made her way into the tiny bathroom.

Locking the door, she took what was probably the fastest shower on record. Drying off just as fast, she quickly got dressed, ran a comb through her hair and was out, rejoining Caleb in what served as a kitchen in a little longer than it took her to make breakfast.

He had just put away the last of the dishes when she walked back in. "Done?" he asked.

"I didn't want to keep you waiting," she explained.

"Waiting? Are you even dry?" he questioned, amazed at the speed with which she had gotten ready.

"I'm dry," she assured him, then put out her arm. "See for yourself."

"I believe you," he said, although he had to admit that he was tempted to slide his fingers along her skin, but for an entirely different reason.

He was being punchy, Caleb chided himself even as he felt himself responding to Nadine. That was what he got for not sleeping most of the night.

Still, there had been times when he had managed to push on for two days straight. That shouldn't really be slowing him down, Caleb thought.

"You finished the dishes," she noted, looking at the rack in the sink.

"I said I would," he reminded her. "Well, if you're all set, I guess we can get going," he told her.

"I thought you said you didn't give your mother a specific time."

"I didn't, but she's an early riser like me so there's no point in wasting any time. Got everything you need?"

She nodded. "Just let me get my coat."

He stood back, out of her way, thinking that she really was a rare woman.

And that, along with other things he was learning about her, made Nadine truly special.

Chapter 9

Nadine was vaguely aware that 201 Richland Avenue, the Colton family home, was in a subdivision of Green Valley and located approximately ten miles west of the city. But since it was so out of the way, she had never had an occasion to drive past the imposing two-story house.

She could hardly take her eyes off it as the building drew closer and closer into view. It brought new meaning to the word *large*.

"That's where you and your brothers and sisters grew up?" she asked incredulously when she finally found her voice.

"Pretty much," Caleb answered casually as he approached what to him was the familiar, rambling wood-and-stone building. He thought it probably appeared somewhat dated to her. "My father had it built for the family a few decades ago, and for the most part, it's been stuck in that era. Although," Caleb continued, "my siblings and I all chipped in to make some renovations. We modernized the kitchen and the connecting family room for Mom for her sixtieth birthday.

"There's an underground parking garage," Caleb said, "but we're not going to be staying here that long, so I'm just going to leave the car out front— unless you'd rather I parked it there," he offered, looking at Nadine for her input.

Nadine had no idea how his mother would react to having her here, so in her opinion, parking the vehicle out front made leaving the premises a little easier.

"No, out front will be just fine," Nadine assured him. "You know," she said as she got out on the passenger side, "it's really none of my business, but you never explained why you were stopping at your mother's."

Was it something important, or something he just routinely did, and did that mean that this handsome attorney was, at bottom, actually a mama's boy? Nadine realized that Annie had left those kinds of details vague when it came to her ex. The only thing she knew for sure was that Annie felt that Caleb was a decent, dedicated man who was always taking off in order to right his father's wrongs, but being one did not necessarily rule out the other.

Caleb paused to think for a moment and realized that she was right. He hadn't told her why they were swinging by. "We all have such busy lives now, I like checking in on her so she doesn't feel quite alone." He didn't mention that he had been by yesterday or that something she had said had prompted this visit on his part.

"Aren't there twelve of you?" Nadine asked. Surely someone in the family had to pop up once in a while, she thought.

Caleb laughed. "I know. It doesn't make much sense, does it? But I'm the oldest and I guess that makes me feel kind of protective of everyone else, especially my mother," he admitted. "Mom still works occasionally," he went on to tell Nadine as he unlocked the rather imposing front door.

His mother worked. She recalled hearing that Isadora Colton was in her seventies. Obviously there were a lot of questions she had neglected to ask Annie, Nadine thought.

"Doing what?" she asked Caleb, curious.

"She's a freelance graphic artist," he answered. Holding open the door for her, Caleb followed Nadine into the house.

Awed, she glanced around the mansion. She couldn't help thinking that it looked to be every bit as huge on the inside as it appeared to be on the outside. Nadine realized that she could have easily fit three of the houses that she had grown up in inside of Caleb's so-called "childhood" home.

"Mom, I'm here," Caleb called out. "Where are you?"

There was no immediate response. "Maybe she went out," Nadine suggested.

But Caleb shook his head. "No, it's too early for her to be out," he told her. He began to investigate the immediate area. "She's around here somewhere. Mom?" he called again.

This time he heard Isa answer from close by.

"I'm looking for my keys. Again," his mother said. She sounded exasperated as she walked into the front room.

Nadine turned toward the woman to get a better look. Caleb's mother was not what she had expected. Looking years younger than her actual age, Isadora Colton was an attractive blonde, with shoulder-length hair, blue eyes and a curvy figure.

But the woman's looks were not the most compelling thing about Caleb's mother. That honor belonged to the baby the woman had tucked in the crook of her arm.

Speechless, Nadine looked at Caleb, a very obvious question in her eyes. She sincerely doubted that Caleb's mother was running a daycare center.

Meanwhile, she was looking at her oldest born for answers to her own questions. When none were immediately forthcoming, Isa switched fronts.

"Hello?" Isa said in greeting, her sky blue eyes sweeping over the young woman at her son's side. "And you are?"

"Very confused right now," Nadine confessed genially.

Swaying slightly to keep the baby she was holding from beginning to cry, Isa looked back at her son. "Caleb?" she asked. "You're the one with all the answers—except when it comes to the whereabouts of my keys," she qualified, looking around the room again.

"Sorry," Caleb apologized. "Mother, this is Nadine Sutherland." He nodded toward the woman who had become his latest project. "Annie's cousin," he added. "Annie thought I could help her." And then he reversed the introduction. "Nadine, this is my mother, Isadora Colton. And that little person she's holding in her arms is my niece, Iris."

"My *only* grandchild," Isa pointedly emphasized, her eyes meeting Nadine's. "Hard to imagine, isn't it?" she asked.

The next moment, Caleb's mother clarified her point. "All those children and you'd think there would be at least a few more grandchildren, wouldn't you?" Isa deliberately looked at her son. "You would think that the rest of my children would step up and at least give me a few more of these," the woman said, smiling down at the infant she was holding cradled against her hip.

Caleb's mother looked extremely natural that way, Nadine couldn't help thinking.

"One's a good start," she told the woman diplomatically. Coming closer, she looked at the baby, who was waving her hands and gurgling. "How old is she?" Nadine asked.

"This little darling is four months old," Isa answered, looking down into the baby's face. "She belongs to my daughter Rachel."

Things clicked in Nadine's head and she turned toward Caleb. "That wouldn't be Rachel Colton, would it?"

"The County DA." Caleb supplied, nodding his head. "Yes, it would. And Rachel is working, which is why Mother suddenly finds herself in the role of babysitter."

"And loving every moment of it," Isa interjected, smiling broadly at her son.

Caleb had just mentioned that his mother was a graphic artist. Taking care of this infant had to cut into the woman's time. A solution occurred to Nadine.

Turning toward Caleb, she asked, "Why don't you or your sister get a nanny to watch the baby?"

"And hand over Iris to some stranger to take care of?" Isa asked in dismay. "Bite your tongue."

Caleb needlessly told Nadine, "Mother's very maternal."

Isa raised her chin proudly. "After raising twelve kids, I should hope so," she declared. She looked down at her grandchild. "You don't have any complaints, do you, Iris?" she asked, talking to the infant as if Iris understood every word.

Nadine smiled at the baby. The center of the conversation was cooing and seemed to be completely fascinated with her own fist. Iris was attempting to stuff it into her mouth, but for now, she wasn't getting anywhere with her project.

Nadine came to Caleb's defense by pointing out the pluses of the situation. "Iris is a lucky baby to have her grandmother's attention like this. If you had more grandchildren right now, Mrs. Colton, this little one might miss out and not be the center of your attention the way she most obviously is."

Amused, Caleb laughed. "You don't know my mother. She has a gift of making each and every one of her kids feel as if they are the only one in her universe. I'm sure that she would do the exact same thing with her grandchildren, no matter how many she had."

"I would," Isa answered with conviction. She turned her attention back to her firstborn. "So why don't you get busy, young man, and see about giving me one or two of those grandchildren?" she asked.

This was not an unfamiliar conversation. It was one that his mother circled back to with a fair amount of regularity. Caleb answered her the way he always did.

"When I have the time."

He felt it useless to tell his mother—again—that at this point in his life, he thought of himself as being a confirmed, eternal bachelor. He had taken one dive into the marital pool with a wonderful woman, but that had gone terribly wrong. And, he concluded, if he hadn't been able to make it work with Annie, there was no chance that he was going to make it work with anyone else.

Right now, all that went unspoken, although his mother had given him a long-suffering, knowing look just now.

It did not go unnoticed by the third party in the room, but Nadine didn't think it was her place to comment on it, not in front of the woman who had given Caleb birth and whom he so obviously held in such high esteem.

Changing the subject slightly, Isa turned toward Nadine. "Would like to hold her?" she asked, holding Rachel's daughter up to Nadine.

Caleb knew what his mother was trying to do. She was trying to stir maternal feelings within someone she was hoping was more than just a client to him.

He attempted to put a stop to that as tactfully as he could. "She doesn't want to hold Rachel's baby, Mom."

"Why don't you let her answer for herself, dear?" Isa suggested with a wide smile.

Nadine decided that turning Isa down would be seen as being impolite. "I would, thank you." She carefully took Iris into her arms.

Watching Nadine's every move, Isa beamed. "Look at that, Caleb. She's a natural," she pointed out to her son happily.

It was time to retreat before his mother pulled Nadine in any further, Caleb thought. "If everything's all right, Mother, I think that Nadine and I are going to be going now," he told her.

"Really?" Isa asked in disbelief. "But you just got here," she said.

"To check on how you were doing," Caleb reminded his mother. "And you seem to be doing fine. I've got a lot of other things to see to."

Isa shook her head as she took the baby back from Nadine. "You know, sometimes you need to stop and smell the roses, just to remember what they actually smell like," she reminded her son. "All work and no play is not good for you, dear," she added with concern.

That was not the way he viewed what he was doing. "You were the one who taught me how to juggle all those balls at the same time, remember, Mom?" he asked.

"Yes, but I never juggled more than I knew that I could competently catch," she reminded her son. "Remember," she said, turning toward Nadine, "never be so busy that you don't leave a sliver of time for yourself." She looked at the baby in her arms. "Uncle Caleb and his friend are leaving, Iris. Say good-bye."

As if on cue, the infant in Isa's arms made a gurgling noise. Her wide eyes seemed to be focused on her uncle and Nadine.

Nothing seemed to escape his mother, Nadine noticed. Isa smiled at her granddaughter's noises. "I think she likes you," she told her son and Nadine.

Caleb humored his mother. "Uh-huh." Looking at Nadine, he began to usher her toward the front door. "Call me if you need anything," he instructed.

"If you could find things for me, that would be lovely," Isa responded, giving the area another cursory look.

That was when Nadine glanced over at the small side table that was standing adjacent to the front door. There, in plain sight, was a set of keys, lying right in the center.

Tugging on Caleb's elbow, Nadine silently pointed.

Caleb grinned at her. "They are on the hall table, Mom," he called out.

Still holding Iris against her hip, Caleb's mother joined them like a shot. She looked down at the keys as if their appearance was akin to the miracle of the loaves and the fishes. "And so they are." She turned toward the infant in her arms. "What do you think of that, Iris?"

"I think you might need glasses, Grandma," Caleb said in a high voice, pretending to be his niece answering his mother.

"Wise guy," his mother stated affectionately.

"Just stating the obvious, Mom," Caleb answered in an equally affectionate voice. Before leaving, he paused to brush a kiss against his mother's cheek. "I'll see you soon, Mom," he promised.

Isa nodded. "I'll hold you to that." And then she looked at Nadine. "Nice meeting you, dear," she told her.

Nadine couldn't help smiling at Caleb's mother. This morning had been an eye-opener for her.

"Same here, Mrs. Colton. It was a real pleasure."

Lifting Iris's hand, Isa waved good-bye to the visitors. Caleb closed the door behind him. "Let's go," he said to Nadine.

They went down the front steps, away from what Nadine could only think of as a mansion. They made their way toward the car that Caleb had left parked out in front.

Nadine turned toward him just as he opened the passenger door, holding it for her. Just before she slipped into her seat, she smiled at him.

"I like her," she told Caleb with genuine feeling.

Caleb smiled and nodded, closing the door for her. Rounding the hood, he got in on the driver's side.

"I thought you would. Everyone does. My mother doesn't have one nasty bone in her whole body," he confided, starting up the vehicle. Although there was nothing around, Caleb looked over his shoulder before backing out. "After everything that my father wound up putting her through, to this day, she still loves the man," he marveled. "She just let me know the other day."

Nadine could easily see that, she thought. "That goodness of hers just seems to radiate out toward everyone who makes even the slightest contact with her."

Caleb's smile grew larger. Nadine couldn't have said anything better if she had tried, he thought, pleased.

Chapter 10

Settling back in the passenger seat, Nadine was silent for a moment. Caleb had suggested that they get some coffee and was driving them over to a shop in the area.

"You know," she said, turning toward him, "I've got mixed feelings about this whole thing with Rutledge Oil."

"You're going to have to elaborate a little more than that if you want me to understand what you're trying to say," he told her.

Pulling up in front of the coffee shop, they went in. Both of them felt as if they needed a second cup to get them going.

Something else they had in common, he couldn't help thinking as he took their drinks over to a small table by the window.

"Well," Nadine explained, "it's nice to be taken seriously about all this instead of just being viewed as some overly dramatic activist who sees people threatening her behind every shadow and creeping out from under every rock. However, not being taken seriously left me with that small sliver of hope that maybe I *was* overreacting. That the threats that I perceived actually *were* imagined and existed just in my head."

Caleb paused, his hands wrapped around his container of coffee as he thought over the comment she had just voiced.

"In other words, you were hoping that the boogeyman wasn't real," he guessed.

Then, he did understand, Nadine thought happily. "Yes," she exclaimed with feeling.

Much as he hated to burst her bubble, in this case, he had to.

"The only problem here is that this 'boogeyman' *is* real. You weren't the only one who heard him and we both saw the guy following you yesterday," Caleb reminded her.

"Maybe they—he or she," Nadine qualified, although she was more than 80 percent certain the driver following them was a man, "were just doing it to get me to back off or back down," she said. "In the last few weeks, I was pretty much in the oil company's face. With justification, I grant you," she quickly added. "But maybe they still believe I'll back off if they exert enough pressure—and if I do, then they will, too."

He looked at her over the last of his remaining coffee. "Do you plan to back off?" he wanted to know.

Nadine thought for a minute, wanting to be completely honest. And then she sighed. There was only one answer she could give him.

"No. They took away fracking rights under some sort of false pretenses. I can't get him to tell me what those pretenses were, but the fact remains that somehow, Rutledge Oil tricked my father out of his land. They played my father. They *took advantage* of him," she emphasized fiercely, "and I can't just let that happen," she insisted. "I can't just allow him to believe that he allowed fracking rights to family land to just be taken away from him like that."

Impassioned, Nadine leaned over the table to make her point. "There has to be some way I can get them for him." Sitting back in her chair again, she concluded, "That's why I need your help."

Caleb couldn't help thinking that the case certainly didn't look winnable on the surface. The fact was that Nadine's father had signed over fracking rights to fifty acres to Rutledge Oil and it apparently looked as if he had done it of his own free will. Proving otherwise was going to be difficult and tricky, to say the least.

"The best way to do that," Caleb told her, "would be proving that your father wasn't of sound mind when he signed over the rights to his land. Then you'd have a good chance of taking the oil company to court, saying that they managed to get the rights to that property by taking advantage of a man who was not in a position to be able to do his own negotiating. I'm going to need to see the paperwork he signed as soon as possible."

"I can get that for you. My father said he had it." But Nadine shook her head, stopping him before he could continue. "But saying my father wasn't of sound mind at the time would be tantamount to saying that he wasn't in full command of his faculties," she pointed out, upset for the man.

Caleb raised his shoulders in a half shrug. He would have put the matter more delicately, but that was the unvarnished bottom line. "In a manner of speaking," he agreed.

"I just can't do that to him," Nadine objected. "Even if it's true," she added unhappily. "Can't you see? If I allowed that to go on record and have everyone know, that would just kill my father. There's got to be another way." Her eyes were literally begging Caleb. "Please."

He felt sorry for Nadine and understood where she was coming from, but at the same time, he felt as if his back was up against a wall. Still, he felt he needed to at least try to find a way out of this dilemma for her.

"Offhand, I don't see how it wouldn't come out about your dad," he admitted, "but—" Just then, Caleb's cell phone rang. "Excuse me for a minute," he said, taking out his phone. He glanced at the number on the screen. "I've got to take this," he told her, getting up from the table. He walked away a few steps.

Perturbed, Nadine took another sip of her coffee. She glanced out the window as she did so. She wasn't really looking at anything in particular, but then she froze.

There was a car cruising down the street at a steady pace. A silver sedan that looked exactly like the one that had been following them yesterday before Caleb had employed those evasive maneuvers he had told her he had learned from a former secret service agent.

Nadine felt her breath backing up in her lungs. The car she had observed drove away from the coffee shop. The pace never picked up.

Was the driver looking for them?

For *her*?

Or was it just some awful coincidence that had

a similar-looking vehicle driving in their immediate area?

She didn't really believe in coincidences.

She wasn't safe, Nadine thought. She had just started to relax, to feel safe again, and now she realized that she had just been fooling herself. There was a target on her back and these people weren't the forgiving type.

They certainly weren't going to back off and walk away.

Caleb returned to their table just then, putting his cell phone into the upper pocket of his suit jacket.

"That was one of the firm's investigators," he told her, taking his seat again. "The one I have looking into people who were contesting Rutledge Oil's tactics."

Nadine read between the lines. "I'm not going to like this, am I?"

"No," he said honestly. "I know I don't. It seems that Rutledge Oil is known for harassing anyone who goes up against them."

"Define 'harassing,'" Nadine requested. "Exactly what does that mean in this case?" She could feel her stomach sinking.

"It means that, for one thing, you're not exactly alone in this." He did see that as a good thing. That meant that the oil company was spreading itself thin in trying to fight everyone. It also meant that they were bound to make a mistake.

"There are multiple pending lawsuits against Rutledge Oil. The bad thing," he continued, "is that several of those have just 'gone away' after the person suing the company was involved in an accident or just managed to disappear." Caleb's expression became totally serious. "I don't want that happening to you. I'm not about to have you become another statistic in this war against the oil company."

She was grateful for his display of protectiveness, but that still didn't change the basic situation.

"What do you suggest?" He was probably going to say something about hiring a real bodyguard, but she couldn't afford to do anything like that.

Her mind immediately began searching for something that she *could* do. Nadine wasn't prepared to hear Caleb say "I want you to come stay with me."

Nadine was grateful that she wasn't drinking her coffee just then, because she was certain she would have started choking.

She looked at him wide-eyed. "You're kidding, right?"

But the stern look on his face told her that he wasn't.

"Hear me out," Caleb requested before she could turn him down. "The penthouse I live in has supertight, around-the-clock security. There is an underground garage beneath the penthouse that has its own security system. And even more important than that, I implicitly trust everyone who surrounds me. Santa Claus couldn't be safer at the North Pole than you would be in my place," he guaranteed.

Nadine sighed.

Her initial reaction to that sort of a suggestion would be to say no—or it would have been before she saw that car, which looked as if it had been circling the area just before Caleb returned to their table.

The same car, she could have sworn, that had been following them—or at least her—yesterday before Caleb wound up spending the night on her sofa.

She caught her lip between her teeth, conducting an internal argument with herself. Agreeing to allow Caleb to take her to his penthouse wouldn't be tantamount to displaying weakness on her part. If anything, she would be showing good sense. After all, she wouldn't have come as far as she had by being just a stubborn fool, she told herself.

Relenting, she surrendered.

"Do you have a spare bedroom?" she asked Caleb, her voice coming across as being exceedingly cautious.

"I have *two* spare bedrooms," he answered, relieved that he wasn't going to have to argue her into this. "You can have your pick."

She still wasn't 100 percent won over. "And how long am I supposed to stay?" Nadine wanted to know.

He didn't know. He didn't have a pat answer for her, certainly not one he knew that she wanted to hear.

"Why don't we take it one day at a time?" Caleb suggested.

Nadine rolled the matter over in her head for a moment, but she knew that she really didn't have a choice here. While it was true that she could get emotionally caught up in her undertakings, she definitely was not reckless.

"All right," she reluctantly agreed. "I'll come and stay at your place. But I'm going to have to stop at my loft first to get a few changes of clothing," she told him, "as well as my jewelry-making tools." She saw the look of surprise pass over his face.

"You want to make jewelry?" he asked, astonished that she could concentrate at a time like this.

She needed something that could take her mind off the immediate circumstances.

"I don't like to waste time." Then she added with a smile, "It's against my religion."

He had no idea if Nadine was kidding or serious. Either way, he already knew the woman didn't like wasting time and he could understand that. He believed in utilizing every second of every day himself.

"Wouldn't want you doing that," he responded.

Thinking the situation over, Caleb told her, "I can have someone go by your loft and get your possessions for you."

He thought that it might be safer that way. Caleb wasn't worried about himself, but he felt that Nadine was already walking around with a bull's-eye firmly attached to her back. He didn't want her out there like that.

"And have some stranger go rifling through my stuff?" she asked, appalled by the thought. "No thank you. I'll pass. I'd rather get my own stuff."

He supposed he could understand why she might feel that way about having an investigator packing up her things. He thought of another solution. "I could have one of my sisters swing by and do it for you."

She shot that down as well. "Right, like they have nothing better to do," Nadine said.

That was all she needed, to have his family think of her as some pampered diva who got herself into trouble and then needed to have her hand held as well as her clothes packed. Well, that certainly wasn't the impression she wanted to create.

Besides, that wasn't the real her, she thought. She hadn't needed hand-holding since she'd been a first grader. Although she liked the idea of the Colton family—and Caleb especially—caring about her.

"That's all right," Nadine assured him, dismissing this suggestion as well. "There's no need to bother anyone or get anyone else involved. It would really be a lot faster if I just went over to the loft and packed everything myself."

"Faster, maybe," Caleb allowed. "But my way would be safer for you."

Nadine sighed. She was not ready to give in. "Tell you what. Let's just agree to disagree," she told Caleb. "In the time that we've just spent disagreeing about this, we could have already gone over to my loft and packed up the necessary things."

The woman was impossible, he thought. Talk about an immovable object.

"Tell me, do you get a kick out of arguing?" he asked.

She didn't answer his question directly. "I like keeping my mind active," she answered. "And we wouldn't even have to be debating this if you had let me get my car from your firm's parking lot," she pointed out. "I could have just driven over to my place myself."

Caleb sighed, shaking his head. "Well, that answers my question."

He had lost her there, Nadine thought. "What question?" she wanted to know, not aware that there was an unanswered question on the table.

"You *do* like to argue," Caleb concluded.

She contradicted him on that point, too. "No, I don't," Nadine insisted. "But I don't back off if I'm right," she stressed. "Now, can we *please* go and get some of my things before the seasons change?"

Caleb surrendered. "Well, if I can't talk you out of it, let's get this over with," he agreed.

All in all, Caleb had to admit that he was surprised at how quickly Nadine could move once they pulled up to her loft. True to her word, she quickly grabbed several necessary items and threw them into her suitcase. Because it was a cloth suitcase, and consequently flexible, she was able to stuff a great deal into it.

He noticed that she wasn't one of those fussy people who insisted on neatly folding each item before turning to the next one. Instead, clothing items all but rained into the suitcase, one after another, followed by a number of undergarments and a couple of pairs of shoes as well.

The entire process from entry to zipping up her suitcase took all of approximately twenty minutes.

Her jewelry-making tools went into another, specially made case.

"Okay, I'm done," Nadine announced, one suitcase in her hand. The jewelry-making bag was hanging off her shoulder, balancing out her purse, which was on the other.

Caleb crossed the floor and took her larger suitcase from her. "I have to say I'm impressed."

"I told you," she said with a broad, satisfied smile.

Yes, he thought, gesturing for her to wait and let him go out of the converted warehouse first, she certainly had.

And, he was beginning to learn, Nadine Sutherland was also a woman of her word.

Chapter 11

Caleb's eyes quickly swept over the sidewalk outside the warehouse, making sure there was no one hiding close by, ready to threaten Nadine—or worse.

But everything looked relatively empty. Still, he was not about to take any unnecessary chances. Caleb quickly waved Nadine over to his vehicle, placing himself between her and any possible trigger-happy hitman who might be looking to take her out.

"You really think they might be lurking around, ready to do something in broad daylight?" Nadine asked him once she had gotten inside.

He gunned his car and quickly left the area. "Yes," he confirmed without any emotion, "I do."

Leaving Nadine's loft behind them, Caleb checked his rearview mirror again to make sure they were not being followed.

They weren't.

At least for now.

But that didn't mean that he was planning to relax his guard.

"All right," he announced when he had put a little distance between them and her loft, "you have a choice to make."

"Ah, more choices," Nadine responded cryptically. This couldn't be good. "What is it?"

"Well, I can either take you to my penthouse apartment where you can settle in while I get back to the office to finish up some work..." Caleb began.

Nadine felt as if she had just been completely wound up, only to be disappointed. The thought of going to his place to put her things away and then spending the remainder of the day waiting for him to come back didn't sound all that appealing to her. And she felt too agitated to concentrate on making those earrings for her client. Inspiration didn't just pop up on demand.

But it sounded as if there were two choices. The second one had to be better than the first, she thought. "Or?" she asked, waiting for Caleb to continue.

"Choice number two is a little more complicated," he explained, attempting to ease into it.

Was he going to make her crawl down his throat and pull the words out of him?

"I'm listening," she told him a little less patiently.

Well, here goes nothing, Caleb thought. If he was going to help her, he needed to do this. "I need to talk to your father."

Nadine thought of the last time that she had attempted to communicate with her father. He had not been having one of his better days. Her father had been short-tempered and everything he'd said to her—when he did talk—had bordered on being downright nasty.

At the time, she consoled herself with the realization that this wasn't really the man she knew. Al Sutherland had never exactly been one of a warm kind of men, but he had never been knowingly nasty, either, not to her.

This was the dementia doing this to him, she thought. The disease was responsible for wiping things out of his memory.

Whenever he realized that something was wrong—and that was happening more frequently these days—her father would lash out at the people whose very presence made him realize that there were facts and events that were missing.

Keeping this in mind, Nadine turned toward Caleb. "I really don't think that's a very good idea," she told him.

But Caleb was not about to close the door on that option just yet. If he was going to be of any use in the fight with the oil company, he needed to meet with Nadine's father.

"I'll be the judge of that."

She felt herself growing defensive as well as being protective of her dad.

"You don't have enough facts to be able to judge things when it comes to my father." With effort, she did her best to make him understand. "Caleb, the man is barely hanging on as it is. If you start asking him about things that he finds himself not being able to call up or even vaguely remember, that could wind up pushing him over the brink."

Caleb saw things differently. "Or," he said, "it just might stir up something for him that he had unwittingly buried in his mind. Something he had been coerced into doing that he hadn't wanted to do, so he just let the event fade from his memory to the point that, for him, it no longer existed. That way, your father wouldn't be tortured by it."

She looked at Caleb, impressed at his reasoning, despite herself. "I thought you said that you were an attorney, not a psychiatrist."

Caleb smiled at her observation. "At one point or another, attorneys have to be all things to their clients. I've played a whole variety of roles for the people who my own father had wound up wronging in his last decade on the bench."

She nodded. For a man with his integrity, having to deal with what Ben Colton had done had to have been very hard on Caleb. "I guess you had a lot of wounds that you had to heal."

"To say the least," he agreed. "But what I'm saying is that puts me in a unique position to be able to understand your father—and you when it comes to him," he added. He saw the wary expression on Nadine's face. "Don't worry. I can be very gentle when I have to be," Caleb promised her.

Her eyes met his for a brief moment. She was searching for an unspoken guarantee. She supposed she had known all along that Caleb would have to get his way when it came to this.

"I will hold you to that," Nadine warned.

He smiled as he looked back at the road. "I'd expect nothing less of you," he answered.

Blowing out a breath, she relented just as she knew she had to. "All right, you can talk to my father. But the second he starts to become agitated, I want you to promise me that you'll back off. If you need to, you can come back and try to talk to him again at another time," she told Caleb. "Deal?"

"Deal," he agreed, knowing that he had no real choice in the matter. But he had to admit that this was better than he had hoped for. He had been prepared to go a few verbal rounds with her before this matter was settled between them.

"The oil company told my father that he could remain on his property for now, but once they start the fracking process—which they said would be very soon—he would have to get out. I'm assuming that the oil company thought that would keep my father docile and not have him create any problems."

Nadine smiled to herself. "My father can be quite a handful at times," she confided.

"Yes, I remember," Caleb responded.

"Oh, that's right," she recalled. "You said you had met him back in the day."

"It was just the one time," Caleb stressed. "But even so, he left quite an impression."

She had no doubt about that. "My father was always rather outspoken," she confirmed.

Caleb glanced in Nadine's direction. "I guess that it runs in the family."

Nadine kept her eyes straight ahead. "I'll pretend I didn't hear that."

"But—" Caleb was about to tell her that he hadn't

meant that as an insult, but she didn't give him a chance.

"Trust me. It's better that way for you," she told him, then explained, "I need to be in a positive frame of mind when I'm dealing with my father. Trying to talk to him can be a very draining experience. Sometimes, he can be just fine—as fine as he used to be, at any rate." *Cheerful* was not a word that had ever been used to describe Al Sutherland. "And other times," she continued, "he turns into someone who I just don't recognize. And to be honest, I don't think he even recognizes himself."

Caleb nodded. "I hate making you do this," he confessed. After all, she had enough to deal with as it was, but he honestly thought his talking with her father might be helpful to the situation. "But I did meet him that one time and who knows? Seeing me again just might spark something in his brain," Caleb told her. "The onset of dementia works in very strange ways," he added, recalling what he had learned about the disease.

"Ah, I see that the psychiatrist is back," she quipped.

He was determined not to take offense. "Just giving you the benefit of all the research I've done."

She looked at his profile. "You researched dementia because of my father?" she questioned. Just how thorough was this man?

"No, I researched it because of a family member of one of my father's victims. Long story," he said, not about to get into the particulars at the moment.

But Nadine wasn't about to be put off that easily. "You need to tell it to me someday," she said, then added, "I think I'd really like to hear one story."

Caleb spared her another glance, after first looking into his rearview mirror again, making sure that they were still not being followed.

So far, so good, he noted.

"First, I need to see your father," Caleb told her, getting back to the reason they were out here.

She nodded. "Right. We're almost there. You've been driving on family land for a few minutes now." At least, she thought, she *hoped* it was still family land. "This was once fifty acres of prime real estate," she recalled nostalgically.

Nadine gestured out the window. "This was all once used for farming. And then my father switched gears, using the land for cattle grazing. Until there were no more cattle to graze.

"After that, the land just sat there, empty and unused—until it was discovered that there was oil running underneath it. That was when my father announced that he was going to explore the idea of doing fracking on the property."

She sighed. Someone should have sat on him or

made him understand that he couldn't just tell everyone about fracking.

"I guess he must have mentioned it to the wrong people. In any case, I didn't hear any more from him until—" Nadine paused, taking a breath, as if that would somehow protect her from the unwanted effects that bad memory might create "—until my father said something about the oil company telling him that he was going to have to move once they started fracking.

"You can imagine how I felt hearing that. When I tried asking my father about it, he got really angry and lashed out. That's when I knew they had to have tricked him out of his fracking rights on his land. Rutledge Oil is not exactly known for being upstanding when it comes to conducting business," she told Caleb bitterly.

Just then, she stopped and pointed to what looked as if it had once been a very well built, moderate-sized house, but time and weather had taken their toll on it.

"That's the house," she announced, pointing to it. "Right there."

Caleb blinked. He hadn't expected the building to appear this run-down. But he did his best to hide his reaction.

"You grew up here?" he asked her, drawing close to the two-story building.

"I did," she told him. "When you're a kid, you don't see the flaws and all the work that needs to be done. It's just home. I've tried to get Dad to move in with me. I do have all that room. But he won't hear of it. This is his home. Which is why I'm worried about what the oil company might do to get him off the land," she confessed.

This much he could do for her right off the top, Caleb thought. "You don't have to worry about that. I can arrange to have some protective custody for him. For both of you," he amended, looking at her pointedly.

"Get it for my father. I can take care of myself."

They were back to that again, he thought. The woman had to stop thinking of herself as some superheroine.

But he wasn't about to argue with her about that now. "We'll talk after I speak with your father."

Nadine nodded. Something to look forward to, she thought sarcastically.

"All right, let's get this over with." She paused for a moment to look at him. "Just don't expect too much," she warned.

And then she rang the doorbell to let her father

know that there was someone at the door. The next moment, she used her key to enter.

Nadine found her father sitting in the small living room. The wiry man immediately rose to his feet and looked at her sharply.

"What are you doing here?" Al Sutherland demanded. "And who's this?" he wanted to know, glaring at Caleb.

Nadine did the introductions. "Dad, this is Caleb Colton. You've met him before," she told her father gently.

Al Sutherland cocked his head, staring at Caleb. The latter had stepped forward and put out his hand.

Al deliberately ignored it. "No, I haven't," he insisted.

Still keeping his hand out, Caleb smiled at the older man. "It was a few years ago, sir," he said politely. "At the time, I had just married your niece, Annie."

"Annie," Al repeated. It was obvious that he was attempting to summon an image to go with the name. And then his expression brightened just a little. "Oh, yes. I remember," he said.

Whether it was the meeting or Annie he remembered wasn't clear to Caleb, but he left the matter alone.

Nadine was fairly certain that her father *didn't* remember. But it was one of those things that could very well pop up in his brain at a later moment, so she didn't want to press the matter.

"How is Annie?" Al asked the newcomer.

Nadine caught Caleb's eye, moving her head slightly. Caleb picked up her cue to keep silent and backed away from the topic, simply saying, "She's fine, sir."

"Good," Al pronounced, nodding his head. And then he looked at his daughter and the man she had brought with her, invading his territory. He grew defensive. "So what are you doing here?" he asked again.

"I came to ask you about Rutledge Oil," she told her father, feeling as if she was cautiously picking her way through a minefield.

She and Caleb were both surprised when her father met her response with a self-satisfied smile.

"Yeah, I really put one over on those guys."

Nadine could feel her stomach tightening, but she managed to keep her expression from reflecting how she felt about her father's claim.

In a light voice, she asked, "How did you do that, Dad?"

Al laughed. "I know that everyone thinks I'm just a bumbling fool, but I got those big dumb idiots to pay for all the fracking costs, and they're going to be giving me a percentage of the profits," he all but crowed gleefully. "You know what that means, don't you?" he asked his daughter.

"What does that mean, Dad?" she asked, doing her best not to allow the dread she felt to come out in her voice.

"That means I'll have something to leave you when I die," Al Sutherland answered.

Chapter 12

"Mr. Sutherland, did I understand you correctly?" Caleb began cautiously. "You said that you are going to be given a percentage of the profits that the oil company will earn by conducting fracking on your property." Caleb watched the older man's face carefully as he waited for an answer.

Nadine's father looked annoyed as well as impatient. It was clear that he didn't like being questioned.

"Guess there's nothing wrong with your hearing," he said sarcastically. "Yes," he confirmed, "that's what I said."

Caleb continued, trying not to make the man feel

as if he was being interrogated. "By any chance, did you sign a contract with them to that effect?"

"Of course I signed a contract," Nadine's father said indignantly, resenting the implication. "I'm not stupid, you know."

Nadine jumped in, running interference. "No one said you were stupid, Dad. We're just trying to get all the facts straight." She knew what Caleb's next question had to be, so she beat him to it and asked her father, "Would you happen to have a copy of that contract?"

Instead of answering her, Al Sutherland jumped to his feet and left the room without saying a word.

Nadine had no idea if her father had just decided to retreat from the conversation or if there was another reason he had departed so abruptly.

After a few minutes had passed and her father hadn't returned, Nadine looked at Caleb. "Maybe I should go after him," she said, at a loss to interpret this latest turn of events.

Before Caleb could answer her or speculate why her father had disappeared like that, Al Sutherland came back. He was carrying a rather large number of what appeared to be bound papers that had been stuffed into a folder.

"Here," he declared dramatically, tossing the folder onto the table. "That's the contract," he added anticlimactically.

The paperwork wound up landing on the floor as well as on the table. Nadine stared at the disorganized storm that went everywhere. Her first reaction was a very strong feeling of being overwhelmed.

Stooping down to pick up the pages that had landed on the floor, she did what she could to pull them all together. Right now, the contract was in desperate need of being organized, she thought. No easy feat by any means.

She looked from the pile of pages to her father. "Did you read this?" she asked him. She honestly didn't know if he was going to boast that he had and bluff his way through it or if he was just going to wave away her question.

Her father did the latter.

"Too many pages," he informed his daughter, looking at her accusingly. "You know that too much reading gives me a headache," he said, annoyed.

"Why didn't you call me?" she asked, trying her best not to make him think she was accusing him but just gently trying to understand what he had to have been thinking. "I would have gone over the contract for you."

Her father narrowed his eyes. He looked obviously offended that she was even asking such a question.

"I already told you," her father insisted, insulted. "This was supposed to be a surprise."

Nadine looked back at the mass of pages piled

up on the table now. She was really afraid that she would discover that her worst fears would turn out to be true.

"It certainly is," she murmured under her breath.

Anger creased her father's features. "I did it for you," her father pointed out, apparently forgetting he had already said as much a few minutes ago.

"I know, Dad. I know," she replied gently. She had not realized that her father actually cared that much about her, and while she was very grateful as well as surprised to be confronted with proof that her father did have such strong feelings about her, she was also devastated and at a loss as to how to get the fracking rights reverted back to him.

"Mr. Sutherland," Caleb interrupted, "would you mind if I took the contract to my law office so I can review it?"

Nadine's father didn't answer right away, as if he was thinking about what Caleb had just proposed. Chewing on his lower lip, he looked from his daughter to this man she had brought with her. His expression was utterly unreadable.

"You'll bring it back, right?" Sutherland finally asked Caleb.

"Absolutely," Caleb promised.

Nadine's father exhaled loudly, as if each word cost him. "Okay, I guess it's all right," he slowly agreed.

The next moment, the older man was scooping up all the loose pages and then unceremoniously thrusting them into Caleb's arms.

"You won't forget?" Sutherland asked, his dark eyes piercing Caleb's.

"No, sir, I definitely won't forget," Caleb promised.

Nadine's father frowned slightly, as if what he was about to say caused him some pain. "All right, take them," he declared, waving for Caleb to leave his home.

It was obvious to both Nadine and the man she had brought with her that their interview with Al Sutherland was officially over.

Rising, Nadine paused as she brushed a quick kiss on her father's wrinkled, pale cheek. "I'll see you soon, Dad," she promised.

Al responded with something that sounded suspiciously like a grunt and then just walked away from both of them.

Caleb left the weathered old house right behind Nadine.

"I'll look this over," Caleb said once they were back in his car and he had placed the contract on the back seat behind the driver. "But offhand, my guess is that there aren't going to be any surprises. I'm pretty sure that your father was tricked into signing away his rights. The promise that his signing the contract would earn him a percentage of the profits from fracking most likely is entirely unsubstantiated. I really doubt that what he believes to be the terms of the contract is reflected anywhere in all those pages." He nodded toward the folder in the back seat.

He wasn't giving voice to anything that hadn't already crossed her mind and turned her stomach into one giant, painful knot.

"Yes," she admitted with a heavy heart, "that's what I'm thinking, too." Nadine turned in her seat to look at Caleb. "If that turns out to be the case, they just can't be allowed to get away with it," she cried passionately.

"No," Caleb answered without any hesitation, "they can't."

He paused for a moment, choosing his next words carefully before continuing. He knew Nadine was going to be upset. She had already indicated as much. But she had to see that this was the most logical path.

"The best—and fastest—way to get the rights back is to have your father declared mentally incompetent." Caleb saw her stiffening, but he pressed on. "That means stating that he was not in his right mind at the time that he signed the contract. I can have his doctor examine him and then make a statement. Or, if he doesn't have a doctor on record, I could get a court-appointed doctor to examine your father." Caleb was confident that the result would be the same. "He's obviously slipping into dementia.

The only question that remains to be asked—and verified—is how far and how fast he had already descended."

Nadine closed her eyes. He could see tears seeping through her eyelashes.

When she opened her eyes again, she told Caleb, "There has to be another way. Now that you've met him, you *know* an admission of that sort would just rip his heart out. If nothing worse, he would be humiliated. And maybe a lot more," she added in a low, morose voice.

Nadine rallied. "There has *got* to be another way. Especially now that he said that his motivation to do what he did was so he could leave me something after he was gone—as if I cared about the money," she concluded dismissively.

Caleb sighed. There didn't seem to be a way out right now. "Your father obviously thinks that you do."

"Well, he got that wrong, too," Nadine informed him. "Caleb, he's slipping further and further away from me, away from the life he's lived. I just can't let this be the last thing that goes down between us."

He nodded. Caleb knew exactly how she had to feel. In his own way, because of his own losses and his dad's misdeeds, he could identify with what Nadine was experiencing.

So he nodded. "All right, I'll go through the contract with a fine-tooth comb and see if there are any options open to us. And I'll see if there's any more information I can gather on the oil company that we can use. Maybe I can find an answer there," he told her.

"I can't thank you enough," Nadine said with feeling.

"No," he agreed, a subdued smile playing on his lips as he thought of what lay ahead of him, "you probably can't."

Caleb's penthouse was just a ten-minute drive from his office. He took her there, thinking that he could just drop her off and go to work. First, of course, he planned to wait for the investigator, who was also a trained bodyguard, that he had called in to show up. He wouldn't be able to concentrate until he was certain that everything was all right because his man was there, watching over Nadine for the sole purpose of keeping her safe.

But if Caleb was hoping to make a quick escape, it would have to wait.

"This is where you live?" Nadine didn't bother to hide the awe in her voice as she looked around, taking in every overwhelming inch.

Caleb had decided to leave his car out in front of his penthouse instead of parking it in the underground garage the way he usually did. He had every intention of taking off as soon as he dropped off Nadine and the luggage she had brought with her—after his investigator showed up, of course.

The line about the best-laid plans of mice and men going astray insisted on echoing through his mind.

"Yes," Caleb answered. "Why?"

"It's absolutely gorgeous," she told him. "And the view…" Her voice trailed off as she stared out through his window. "That's the waterfront," Nadine marveled.

He tried not to laugh. He found her reaction almost endearing. "Yes, I know."

She turned toward him. "If I were you I would definitely find a way to work out of the house so I could just drink all this in."

He shook his head at her suggestion. "I'm afraid that can't be done. As I'm sure that Annie must have told you, my work takes me all over. Sometimes," he admitted, "I hardly even get a chance to touch home base."

Nadine pressed her lips together. Caleb was being extremely kind to her. He was trying to help her father, not to mention taking her into his house because he wanted to protect her. Dwelling on his failed marriage to Annie didn't seem like the right way to repay the man, she thought. She veered away from the subject that he had brought up.

"Well, this is a beautiful home," she told him

with enthusiasm. "Thank you for taking me in, and I promise not to do anything to mess it up in any way."

"I know that," he said.

She turned to look at him, curious. "How? How would you?" she asked.

"Because I saw where you lived," he answered simply. "And how that place was ripe for looking as if a tornado had hit it, and yet everywhere I looked, your loft was incredibly neat."

Still waiting for his man to make an appearance, Caleb smiled as he took her suitcase to the closest bedroom.

"I am confident that I'll be leaving my penthouse in good hands—as soon as Hogan gets here," he qualified, in case Nadine thought he was leaving her alone.

"Hogan?" she questioned. He hadn't mentioned that name to her before.

"Mike Hogan," he told her. "He's one of the firm's investigators. I placed a call to him this morning."

She bristled at the implication that she needed a keeper other than Caleb himself. "Well, my natural inclination is to tell you that you're certainly free to leave right now. You indicated that you regard this penthouse to be a fortress. To me, that means that I'm really safe staying here, even if your investigator was not on his way over.

"But we've already had this conversation and it's

gone nowhere, so I'll be quiet," Nadine concluded, resigned.

Caleb looked at her. Just when he thought the topic had finally been put to rest, Nadine added her unique footnote by saying, "But I just want to go on record one last time that you're hanging around here of your own free will and not because of me."

Caleb could only shake his head. "Duly noted." And then humor curved his lips. "Don't worry. I'm not about to tell anyone that you 'made' me stay and hold your hand until the necessary security detail showed up."

"I don't care what anyone else says or thinks," she informed him. "I just wanted the matter to be clear between us."

The smile on his lips turned into a grin. "Oh, it's very clear," he guaranteed.

Before she could say anything further, Caleb heard his doorbell ring. He instantly looked at the closest monitor to see who was standing on his doorstep.

"Hogan's here," he announced for Nadine's benefit.

"Is this where I clap?" she said.

"You can if you want to," he told her cheerfully, striding past her to open the door.

Mike Hogan looked more like a man on his way to a board meeting than someone who was a private investigator. Tall and solemn looking, he was wearing a three-piece suit beneath the tan overcoat he had on to protect him against the biting cold weather.

"This is Nadine Sutherland," Caleb explained to his investigator.

Hogan took off his overcoat and leaned forward to shake her hand.

"A pleasure, ma'am," he stated her in a soft-spoken voice, then added, "You won't even know I'm here."

He had to say that, Nadine thought, but she didn't bother contesting the investigator's assurance.

Instead, she turned toward Caleb and told him, "I guess that's your cue to leave, Caleb. You're free."

He let her remark pass. "If you think of anything, or need anything, you know where to reach me." The words were addressed to both of the people in the room and hung in the air as he walked out of his penthouse.

Leaving Nadine with Hogan, he thought, was going to be very interesting.

Chapter 13

Caleb walked into his private office and deposited his briefcase on his desk. The tan case was stuffed with all the loose pages that, once put together, supposedly comprised the contract that Al Sutherland said he had signed.

If asked, Caleb couldn't very well say that he was looking forward to emptying his briefcase and having the avalanche of papers come tumbling out onto his desk. But he knew that he had to.

Someday, he told himself, he was going to learn to say no. But then, he thought the next moment, if sacrificing his marriage and two long-term relationships hadn't taught him how to hold some of himself back while involved in conducting an investigation, he sincerely doubted that he was ever going to change his ways.

Flipping open the locks on his briefcase, he opened the lid and looked down at the pile waiting for his attention.

A movement going past his open office door caught his attention and he looked up. Rebekah had nearly made it out of his view when Caleb called out her name.

Dutifully, the assistant retraced her steps and stuck her head into Caleb's office. "Is there something that I can do for you?" Rebekah wanted to know.

"Yes, you can send Morgan into my office," Caleb told the assistant.

Rebekah made no attempt to act on his request. "I would if I could, boss man, but I can't."

Caleb's eyes narrowed as he looked at his employee more closely. "And just why is that?" he asked.

"Because Ms. Colton still hasn't come in today," Rebekah answered simply.

Caleb glanced at his watch. It was close to two in the afternoon.

"I know," Rebekah said, noticing the attorney looking at his watch. She guessed at what he had to be thinking. "It must be nice to come and go as you please."

Caleb didn't say anything about his assistant's comment and just went to the heart of the matter. "Did my sister call to tell you where she was or when she would be in?"

It was obvious that Rebekah found the question amusing. "She doesn't check in with me, Mr. Colton, unless it's to call to find out about something in her schedule. But if I hear anything," the older woman promised him, "I'll be sure to let you know."

Rebekah had just stepped away from his doorway when she suddenly made her way back into his office. He looked at her quizzically.

Never missing a beat, Rebekah announced, "This is me, letting you know that your sister just walked in."

Caleb abandoned his briefcase and the contract he'd been planning to examine. He stepped out into the hallway just in time to practically bump smack into Morgan. The latter was making her way to her own office.

Reflexes had him taking a step back to avoid a collision between them. As he did so, he took a second look at his twin. He was accustomed to Morgan being impeccably groomed. There was never a single hair on her head that was ever out of place.

Until now.

He saw Rebekah looking at him over his twin's head. It was not difficult to read the woman's expression. The assistant was thinking the exact same thing that he was.

There must be something private going on with Morgan, and Caleb was feeling very protective of his twin.

"I'll call you if I need you, Rebekah," he told the assistant, dismissing the woman.

Resigned, Rebekah took her cue and backtracked out of the office.

Turning back toward his twin, Caleb now that Morgan had taken the opportunity to go into her office. Caleb was quick to follow her.

"Are you okay?" he asked, crossing her office threshold.

Morgan dropped her purse on the floor and deposited her body into her office chair in like manner. He noticed that she gripped the armrests before answering.

"Just peachy," Morgan responded sarcastically.

Caleb made no bones about his own reaction to her appearance. "Well, you look like hell."

"Thank you," she retorted icily, then backed off a little. "If I knew what hell looks like, I'd probably agree with you. Do we have any coffee left?" she wanted to know. "Or did you and Rebekah drink it all?" Everyone knew that Rebekah claimed to run on caffeine.

"I've had a busy morning and just got in a little while ago myself, so I think it's safe to assume there's still some coffee available for you. If not, I'll have Rebekah make some. Barring that, I can make you coffee myself," he informed his sister. "But first, why don't you tell me why you look like the human equivalent of thirty miles of bad road?"

Morgan didn't answer her brother immediately. Instead, she paused to consider her response before saying anything. "I might have gone to a friend's birthday party at the Corner Pocket," she told him, mentioning a billiard bar that was located downtown. "Toward the end of the evening, the drinks were flowing like water, and I might have gotten a bit too carried away," Morgan admitted, although not too readily.

Without realizing it, she placed her hand to her forehead, as if she was attempting to contain the pain.

"I could swear that my head is throbbing to some sort of rhythmic beat," she murmured, agitated. Blowing out an impatient breath, she signaled the end of the discussion. "That's all I'm going to say about it for now. So, if you were hoping to hear some sort of a tantalizing confession, you're going to be disappointed," she informed her twin.

"You're here in one piece. There's nothing for me to be disappointed about."

About to leave, Caleb paused and opened the bottom left-hand drawer of his twin's desk. Crouching, he extracted a bottle of aspirin and placed it in the center of her desk, then went over to the sink located in her private bathroom, got a glass and filled it with water.

Retracing his steps, Caleb put the glass next to the bottle of aspirin. "You might want to take a couple of these," he suggested, nodding at the aspirin. "Could help you put a smile on your face," he told her as he turned toward the office door.

Caleb tossed one final thing over his shoulder. "You know where to find me if you want to talk. I should be here for at least another hour."

Resigned, Morgan drew the bottle closer to her. It took her a minute to open the container and then take out two pills. Contemplating them, Morgan took out a third, then swallowed all three.

As she leaned back in her chair, he saw her close her eyes.

Satisfied there wasn't anything further he could do for his sister right now, Caleb withdrew from her office, closing the door quietly behind him.

He and Morgan were usually on the same wavelength, almost eerily so, he thought as he returned to his own office. But there were times when his twin withdrew into herself. While it did arouse his curiosity when that happened, he knew when to leave her alone.

And, he silently argued, when his marriage was beginning to unravel at the seams, he hadn't said anything to Morgan about it for a long time. And then he'd told her only because his divorce looked as if it was going to become a reality. He'd known that his twin would probably feel hurt that he had deliberately shut her out if he didn't tell her about it before it became public news, which was why he'd finally informed her.

That kind of thing was a two-way street. It wasn't traveled often, but when it was, it had to be done very carefully.

Whatever had happened last night to get Morgan to a place where she looked like this the following day, Caleb knew she would eventually tell him. Until then, he would remain supportive from a distance and do his best to keep out of her way.

Heaven knew, he thought, eyeing the stack of papers all but spilling out of his briefcase, he had more than enough to keep him busy. And wading through Nadine's father's contract wasn't nearly the half of it. The firm that he and Morgan ran had expanded since its early days. They didn't just handle cases through the Truth Foundation that involved all those people their father had wrongfully sent to prison.

Caleb settled in to organize the avalanche of papers that comprised the contract between Nadine's father and the oil company. As he did so, he forgot all about the coffee he had meant to get for himself as well as the cup for Morgan.

Three hours went by. In that time, after organizing the profusion of papers and finally getting them all in order, he had managed to read through the contract in its entirety twice. Once to absorb the general gist of it and a second time to make sure that he hadn't managed to miss anything.

He came away with the feeling that whoever had written this document was definitely enamored with the written word, also with finding the most complicated way to state even the simplest of thoughts.

Rutledge Oil, Caleb thought, had tried its best to completely confuse Al Sutherland and, very simply, to put one over on the man. He was convinced that the company had probably told Nadine's father exactly what he wanted to hear, but there was certainly no evidence of that within the actual contract.

What Caleb saw within the contract was that Al Sutherland had sold the fracking rights to his property outright. The monetary compensation for that sale was as small as it could be—for what amounted to a song. And, despite reading the contract twice, he couldn't find any mention of any sort of a percentage being paid on the amount of money that any fracking taking place on the land would yield.

Caleb sighed as he put down the last page. The oil

company was definitely cheating Nadine's father. But at the moment, he had no proof to point to other than what an old man with the onset of dementia creeping into his brain said was the bargain he had agreed to.

Caleb closed his eyes and sighed. Frustrated, he could feel a headache threatening to descend.

There had to be a way around this, he thought. There had to be *something* he could do to get the oil company to back off.

He thought about it. Since Nadine absolutely refused to approach this from the angle that the oil company had taken advantage of a man who was losing his mental faculties, Caleb felt he had only one course of behavior open to him.

He had to find something he could use against the oil company. Caleb knew that it wouldn't be easy, but he was fairly certain that the less-than-upstanding-and-honest executives must have done this sort of thing before.

The very fact that there were so many people suing pointed to that. He was going to be banking on the fact that there had to be at least one case that was similar to Al Sutherland's somewhere in all those pending litigations.

All he had to do was just find one case like that. If he did, he felt certain that that could open up a world of possibilities for Nadine's father.

Caleb smiled to himself. At least he had a sliver of hope to offer to Nadine, he thought.

Before returning to his penthouse—and Nadine—Caleb looked in on his sister. Crossing the threshold, he was pleased to see that Morgan looked as if she was in slightly better shape than when she had first walked in.

The color had returned to her face, and while she still looked a little pale, she was no longer an ashen shade of white.

"I'm leaving now."

Morgan didn't look up. "Okay. I'll see you," she said.

Caleb still hesitated. "You'll be all right?"

This time Morgan did look up as she stopped writing. "When *haven't* I been all right?"

"Oh, I can think of a few times," he said loftily.

A hint of a smile touched her lips fleetingly. He was goading her. That was his way of trying to make her come around. "Go, save the world, Caleb. I'll be all right."

He nodded. "All right. But call me if you need anything."

Morgan had already gone back to writing. "I'll call," she murmured.

As he left the office, Caleb still couldn't help wondering what last night, and consequently, the following day had been all about. Morgan was usually a very "together" woman who wasn't fazed by anything.

Well, his sister would tell him in her own time, he told himself not for the first time. He was well aware that pressing the matter wouldn't get him anywhere. As a matter of fact, he was fairly sure that pressing Morgan would have the exact opposite effect.

Caleb glanced at his phone as he pulled out of his parking space. There didn't appear to be any messages, either text or called in. He hoped that meant that it was "all quiet on the Western front" and that he wouldn't be coming home to any unexpected "surprises."

Even so, he picked up his speed, driving home just under the legal limit. That sort of behavior was ingrained in him. The last thing he wanted was to get a ticket. Not because it would leave a blemish on his perfect driving record, but because being pulled over and waiting for an officer to write him up would eat up more time than he would save by driving fast.

Caleb had learned to be very aware of the consequences that might arise from any sort of action that he undertook. That lesson had been learned by finding out that his father was not the man that everyone had thought him to be for so many years. Caleb had promised himself that, no matter what, he would always lead a good life, so that anyone crossing his path would know that what they saw was what they got.

Anything else, he felt, would just be the height of dishonesty, a blemish that he swore would never touch him.

Chapter 14

Caleb stopped at a nearby restaurant and picked up the dinner he had ordered just before he left his office. Nadine was undoubtedly hungry by now, and in his opinion, the idea of leftovers didn't seem quite the way to go for her first meal at his penthouse.

With the warm, enticing scent of barbecued spare-ribs wafting through the interior of his car, Caleb drove the short distance home.

Arriving at his place, he parked his vehicle in its regular spot in the underground garage. There were security cameras within the space, but he locked his vehicle anyway and made his way up to his penthouse.

He found Hogan inconspicuously planted near the

penthouse's entry. He hadn't expected that the investigator would be outside the living space. When their eyes met, Caleb raised a quizzical eyebrow, silently asking the man why he was out here and not inside.

"I didn't want your lady friend to feel that I was breathing down her neck," Hogan explained. "I felt that she would be more comfortable if she knew I was around, but not necessarily right in her face. Kind of a reversal of that old saying of being seen but not heard. Hope that's all right," Hogan added, looking at his employer.

Caleb had chosen the investigator not just for his expertise but for his sensitivity in various situations as well. He trusted the man's natural intuition. And, of course, there were the security safeguards that had been put in place throughout the penthouse.

"That's fine with me," Caleb assured the other man. "I take it everything has gone smoothly," Caleb said.

"Just like silk," Hogan replied. "If you need anything, I'll be around for the rest of the night. Jacobson will spell me at midnight."

Caleb nodded. That saved him the trouble of calling the other man.

"I appreciate it," he told Hogan. "I'm pretty confident that there's nothing to worry about, but right now, quite honestly, I'd rather err on the side of caution than not."

The investigator looked as if he totally agreed. "Always a good idea," Hogan said. The man was already stepping back into the shadows. "Have a nice evening, sir."

"You, too, Hogan," Caleb replied as he entered his penthouse.

Once inside, he looked around. Everything looked exactly the way he had left it. It didn't even look as if there had been anyone else there, nor did it appear as if anyone was there now. But he knew there had to be. Hogan was far too good at his job for Nadine to have managed to slip out and leave the premises, not that she would have wanted to make good her escape right now.

Besides, he still had the contract that her father had signed in his possession, so even if Nadine had wanted to leave for some reason, she wouldn't have. Not while she needed help in finding a way to make the oil company return the fracking rights to her father.

Still carrying his briefcase and the bag containing their dinner, Caleb made his way into his state-of-the-art kitchen.

She wasn't there, either.

Rather than carry the items around with him through the house, he set them down on the counter.

"Nadine," he called out, "where are you?"

He listened for a response. And that was when he heard it.

Music. It had rather a tinny sound.

It occurred to him that Nadine must have found his old transistor radio. He knew he should have gotten rid of it a long time ago. But he had kept it because it was a holdover from a happier, more innocent childhood. It reminded him of when his father had been his hero and hadn't yet sullied the family name or had been a good man who had time for his wife as well as for all of his children.

Caleb followed the music and it led him into the family room. Nadine was sitting cross-legged on the floor in front of the wide coffee table and she looked to be working. Her jewelry-making tools were all carefully spread out on top of the paper towels she had used to cover the table. She was concentrating on an earring that she was putting the finishing touches on.

Watching her, Caleb crossed into the room. "What are you doing?"

"Well, without anyone to talk to, it got pretty lonely in here," she admitted. She could usually call a friend to talk or go out for a stroll. Neither was possible right now. "I found this cute little radio and I turned it on to keep me company as well as fill up the awful quiet. I didn't think you'd mind," she added as she watched him take the transistor and turn it off. "I guess I thought wrong," she realized. "Sorry."

"Nothing to be sorry about," Caleb responded, then admitted, "I guess I'm a little sentimental about it." He smiled to himself at the memories it brought back and nodded at the radio. "I saw this one day while I was out with my father. I think that I was probably about six at the time. Anyway, being a kid of privilege, I had never seen anything like it and I asked him all sorts of questions about it. He got a kick out of all the things I thought to ask about something that looked so simple to him, so he bought it for me," he told Nadine.

The smile on his face was rather sad, Nadine thought.

"It reminds me of a happier time," Caleb confessed. His eyes met hers. "You probably think that's silly."

"No," she responded in all sincerity. "I think that's sweet. We all need something to hang on to that reminds us of better times," Nadine maintained. "Sometimes, having something to hang on to is all we have to help us move forward."

She said it with such conviction, Caleb knew she had to be thinking of her father. Except that in Al Sutherland's case, there were no better times on the horizon. The best she could hope for was that her father would remain in his present state for a while longer. But they both knew that nothing got better for someone in Sutherland's condition. They just deteriorated.

Caleb's heart went out to her. In an odd sort of way, they shared a kind of darkness that had intruded into their lives and overwhelmed them, even though that darkness had arrived in different ways, he couldn't help thinking.

Their eyes met and he felt this intense desire to comfort her, to find a way to bring a smile back to her face.

He wanted, he realized, to take Nadine into his arms and kiss her.

Wavering, Caleb came very close to doing just that. But at that moment, a rousing song came on the radio and, coupled with the scent of the barbecued spareribs, it proved to be the perfect antidote to the momentary romantic surge that had threatened to wash over him.

Looking into his eyes, Nadine had felt very drawn to Caleb. She had almost gotten carried away.

Nadine took a deep breath, fortifying herself. She clutched at the first thing that presented itself to her.

"What is that amazing smell?" she asked.

Caleb grinned. "I take it you're not referring to my cologne," he told her with a chuckle. "So you're probably talking about the spareribs."

"Sparcribs?" she asked.

"In there," he said, pointing toward the large bag

he had set down on the counter. "I thought you might be hungry, so I stopped by a restaurant on the way home and picked up some spareribs. I was going with my own tastes," he confessed, then apologized, "I didn't stop to think that you might find eating them to be a kind of messy experience."

This man had to be the poster child for the word *thoughtful*, Nadine couldn't help thinking with a smile.

"'Messy' can always wash off. Unless it's the kind of messy that involves the soul," Nadine qualified as she thought of what the oil company had done to her father.

Caleb looked at her. "Glad you have such a positive attitude," he said, adding, "about dinner."

Nadine smiled at him. Then, walking into the kitchen, she looked around. "You wouldn't by any chance have any paper plates, would you?"

He shook his head. "Sorry, no, I don't." Her question aroused his curiosity. "Why?"

Crossing to the counter, he picked up the bag and brought it over to the kitchen table, placing it in the center. He opened it and took out the large containers with spareribs, then flipped open the tops.

"I just thought if you had paper plates, cleanup would go a lot faster. But don't worry," she quickly assured him, "I'll be happy to wash the dishes."

"I wasn't worried," he said, bringing over three

plates, one for each of them and one to place beneath the containers in case they wound up leaking. "And you're not washing anything. That's why dishwashers were created," he added whimsically.

She didn't accept his theory. "Washing dishes is therapeutic," she said.

He had never heard that one before. "Let's eat off those dishes first, then we'll talk about doing something 'therapeutic' with them," he told her. Looking inside the bag, he realized that he had forgotten about the side he had ordered. "How do you feel about potato salad?" he asked her.

Nadine didn't even have to pause to think. "I love potato salad," she freely admitted.

His smile rose all the way up into his eyes. "Good answer, because I picked up some, too." Taking out the large container of potato salad and placing it between the two giant-sized servings of spareribs, Caleb looked at the plates. "Not exactly a meal fit for a king, is it?"

"Well, unless you're hiding him, I didn't see any kings here in your penthouse—unless, of course, you're referring to yourself," Nadine added with a wide smile.

That surprised him. "I wasn't talking about me."

"And you shouldn't be talking like that about the spareribs, either. Because if they taste anywhere as good as they smell, I'd say that I'm going to be in for a *real* feast."

Nadine was being extremely upbeat, he thought. So upbeat, Caleb decided, that he was not going to say anything tonight about the contract that her father had signed. There was no immediate hurry. The discussion could wait until morning. Bad news had a way of keeping, since it wasn't about to go anywhere, certainly not without any sort of constructive help on his part if he was even able to come up with any.

For now, Caleb looked across the table, fascinated as he watched his houseguest eat. She really seemed to enjoy the spareribs, he thought.

Unlike a lot of the women he had known, Nadine wasn't fussy about eating. She dug into her food with gusto, but even so, she somehow managed to make short work of the ribs without getting any of the sauce on herself.

It was a neat trick, he thought.

"I take it that you like them," Caleb concluded, nodding at the quickly disappearing meal.

"Like them?" she echoed. "This is absolutely delicious—and exactly what I need to make me feel like a whole person again." Nadine raised her eyes to his face. "Because," she continued more seriously, "I have a feeling I'm going to need that."

Caleb felt slightly uneasy but told himself that he was probably either just imagining things or reading into her statement, turning it into something she probably didn't intend.

"I don't know what you mean," Caleb responded innocently.

"Oh, I think you do," she said.

There was nothing high-handed in her tone. To her mind, she was simply stating a fact. She had been around enough people to become a fairly good judge of the behavior she witnessed. In Caleb's case, she had found herself becoming a quick study.

Maybe it had to do with the fact that she felt they were going to be working closely together, or perhaps because he had been married to her cousin. Either way, Nadine felt she had some sort of special insight into the man, an insight that exceeded her usual expertise.

Caleb was still hoping that he had jumped to the wrong conclusion. And she appreciated his caring—more than she'd like to admit.

"Enlighten me," he coaxed.

"You left me in your penthouse under the invisible yet watchful eye of your investigator while you lugged off that contract that my father signed, defining his bargain with the oil company. Now you've been home for a while and you still haven't said word one about it.

"The only conclusion I can come to is that you

didn't want me to lose my appetite by giving me any bad news right up front." She paused. "Am I right?"

Caleb laughed dryly, shaking his head. The woman was sharp. She had hit the nail right on the head—as clever as she was attractive.

"You know, if you ever decide you want to switch careers, I'd be happy to take you on as part of my team, working as an investigator. You've got a natural knack for it."

She knew what he was attempting to do. "Thank you, but you're not going to distract me," she told Caleb. Her eyes pinned him down. "What did you find when you went through that fifty-pound contract?"

Cornered, he had to be honest with her. "Not what any of us wanted to find," he said simply.

Her heart sank. She knew what that meant. "My father really did give those rights over to Rutledge Oil, didn't he?"

He didn't attempt to camouflage his words in any way. "Yes."

She might as well know the whole sordid truth, she thought. "And he won't be getting any sort of a payment from the fracking that's going to be taking place, is he?" she asked.

"No, he's not," Caleb told her. "But I am *not* giving up," he quickly reassured her.

She pulled her shoulders back. "I am not going

to have my father humiliated, publicly or privately," she stressed.

"Pending a lawsuit, I'm trying to find another way to get this thrown out of court," he said.

Nadine nodded, relaxing slightly. "All right, as long as we're clear on that point."

He laughed. "I'd have to be a fool not to be clear on that by now."

The comment made her smile. "Well, after knowing you for only a little bit, I can confidently say that you are definitely not a fool," she told him.

With that, Nadine rose, picking up his plate as well as her own and taking both to the sink. "Don't try to stop me," she warned. "I find myself in need of some therapy," she announced.

"I wouldn't dream of stopping you," he said, picking up a dish towel. "I just want to join you."

Smiling, she inclined her head. "By all means," Nadine invited with a wide smile.

Chapter 15

The sound of his ringing cell phone burrowed its way into Caleb's brain, dissolving the remnants of the dream he had been having, instantly driving it from his memory.

Reluctantly opening his eyes, Caleb blinked, focusing on the clock next to his bed. It was almost seven.

Memories played themselves through his head in a backward procession, going from the last thing he recalled to the first. Caleb remembered going to bed after midnight after having stayed up talking to Nadine and going over recent happenings.

He clarified the events for her benefit, although

they weren't about anything that concerned her father. What he had told her about were things that had to do with his father and the host of people Ben Colton had wronged in that final decade that he had sat on the bench as a judge.

The throbbing noise continued.

Caleb suddenly realized that he was ignoring his phone.

Sitting up, he picked up his cell phone, opened it and mumbled "Hello?" in a voice that was still thick with the last remnants of sleep.

"Good morning, Sleeping Beauty," the voice in his ear said. "I gather that I just woke you up."

Caleb immediately recognized Morgan's voice. His twin was obviously trying to make up for yesterday, he thought.

Sighing, he dragged his hand through his hair, then passed that hand over his eyes, doing what he could to get them in focus.

"I had a late night," he muttered by way of an excuse for his present condition.

"Oh?"

He could hear barely contained interest in the single word and knew Morgan was dying to shoot questions at him.

He cut her short.

"No 'oh.' It was work. Now, is there any reason

you're calling so early?" Morgan never called just to shoot the breeze, Caleb thought.

Morgan's voice became businesslike. "As a matter of fact, Caleb, there is. That man called again."

Longing for a cup of coffee, Caleb kicked off his covers. He told Morgan he'd call her right back, jumped in the shower quickly, and after he got out and finished shaving, reached for the pair of pants he had left hanging off the end of his bed.

"You're going to have to get more specific than that," he told his twin after calling her back. "*What* man?"

"Ronald Spence," she answered impatiently. Spence had been the last man their father had sentenced to prison before his death. "I don't know how he gets to make so many phone calls since he's in prison, but the upshot is he still maintains that Dad railroaded him, sending him to prison, and that he's innocent. He's been saying that for the last six months. He swears that Dad actually hid the papers that would have cleared him of the charges against him."

Holding his phone against his ear by using his shoulder, Caleb finally managed to pull on his pants.

He sighed at what Morgan had just said. "Yeah, there was a lot of that going on."

"Spence wants us to find those papers. He's positive they will exonerate him. He told me that he's got a fairly good idea where they might have been stashed."

"Boy, you certainly have been a busy little bee, haven't you?" Caleb remarked. "And the sun's barely up." Grabbing a fresh shirt, Caleb shrugged into it. "I'm assuming you wrote down the specifics Spence gave you."

His twin replied, "Yes, Caleb, I did."

He pulled on his socks, then stuffed his feet into his shoes. "I'll be there as soon as I can," he promised Morgan.

"Did Annie's cousin stay at your place last night?" his sister suddenly asked him out of the blue.

"Yes, she did—and she still is." He knew that was what Morgan was really asking. "I told you, someone was following her. Why do you ask?" he wanted to know.

"I'm just trying to gauge exactly what you meant by saying 'as soon as I can,'" Morgan answered.

"She's Annie's *cousin*, remember?" Caleb stressed, as if that should be all the answer she needed.

He was not prepared to hear his twin chuckle at his answer. "Yes," Morgan responded, "I am familiar with the family."

This was pointless. He could get ready a lot faster without dealing with Morgan's veiled questions and innuendos.

"Later," he said to his twin firmly just before he terminated their connection.

Caleb frowned to himself. Just because Morgan had gone to a birthday party and come into the office late the following day, looking the worse for wear because of her "adventure," didn't mean that he was going to do anything of the kind just because he had taken Nadine under his wing. He had taken her case pro bono, for heaven's sake. Morgan should know that, he thought.

But then, he'd never seen his sister acting so out of character before, either. Working all these hours, trying to right all those wrongs his father had committed while they were still building up and running a profitable law firm was beginning to take its toll on both of them, he thought. And, just when they felt that they may have finally rid their family of all the shame their father's behavior had brought down on them, Ronald Spence suddenly contacted them.

Caleb took a deep breath, intent on centering himself.

Onward and upward, he silently counseled, tucking in his shirt and grabbing a tie and jacket out of his closet.

It wasn't until he was in the hallway that he thought he detected the smell of something cooking.

Afraid that he had left the stove on for some reason, Caleb quickened his pace. He flew down the stairs and reached the kitchen's threshold in what amounted to record time.

That was when Caleb came to an abrupt halt. "You're cooking?" he asked, looking at what Nadine was doing.

"I do know how to cook," she told him. "And since you took me out for dinner one day and then brought me takeout last night, I thought that it was only fair that I turned around and returned the favor this morning."

Looking at him over her shoulder, she studied Caleb. He looked like a man who was in a hurry. "Do you have time to sit down and eat or should I just pack this up so you can take it with you?" she asked.

He stared at her. That was a hell of a guess on her part. "How did you—?"

"I heard your cell phone ringing this morning— sound carries. And then you came right down like you were in a hurry—I could hear your feet hitting the ground as you ran," she explained.

Caleb laughed, shaking his head in wonder as he sat down at the table. He figured he could spare a few minutes to eat, since Nadine had obviously gone through all this trouble.

"Like I said," he said to her, not bothering to hide that she had managed to impress him, "that job on my investigative team is open for you anytime you want it."

Nadine placed his breakfast in front of him, then poured a cup of coffee for him before she duplicated the action for herself. Sitting down opposite Caleb, she made herself comfortable.

"So," she asked her host, "where are you off to in such a hurry so early—or am I not supposed to ask." She gestured to the paperwork. "I found a name in your papers—Ronald Spence. Does this have to do with him, by any chance?"

"Well, you can ask," he began to tell her in between bites, then stopped abruptly as what he had just put in his mouth registered. "This is also really good," he declared, nodding at his plate.

"Don't look so surprised," she told him. "Yesterday wasn't an accident. I've been cooking ever since I was a little girl, right after my mother passed away," Nadine confided. "You said I could ask why you're leaving so early, so this is me, asking," Nadine said, waiting for him to give her an answer.

"You have a mind like a homing device, don't you?" he asked, amused.

Nadine saw no reason to dispute that. "I do, and you're stalling," she pointed out. "Are you planning on telling me, or are you going to shut me out after all?"

The fact that it was none of her business didn't really register with her.

"The former," he said, then got to the heart of

the matter. "The last man my father sent to prison has been calling the office lately, professing his innocence. He's trying to get us to take on his case." Caleb raised his shoulders in a vague shrug. "I thought I should check it out."

"Doesn't your sister work at the foundation, too?" Nadine asked, fairly certain that the answer was yes.

He knew what Nadine was getting at. His protective nature toward his siblings kicked in. "She does, but she's working on something right now."

"And you thought that you'd take on this Spence person's case because you have so much free time on your hands?" Nadine said with a touch of sarcasm.

The laugh that escaped his lips was dry. "You're beginning to sound like my mother," he told her.

"Well, since I've met your mother, I'm flattered." Noticing that Caleb had finished his breakfast, she cleared away his plate. "Anything I can do to help?" she asked.

The offer sounded genuine to Caleb. He had to admit that this woman really intrigued him.

"You're doing it."

He was referring to making breakfast, she thought. But she wasn't. "I mean, with what you're doing," she said, leaving his dish in the sink for now. She returned to the table and was about to sit down, but Caleb had already begun walking toward the door.

"I'll let you know when I get back," he promised.

A thought hit her. "I could come with you," Nadine offered.

"To prison?" Caleb questioned. "That's where I'm meeting Spence," he told her, thinking he would pick up any information he needed when he swung by his office.

"Well, it's not like it would be my first time," Nadine reminded him. "At this point, I could probably give you a tour of our finer holding establishments."

Caleb was about to turn her down, saying that he would feel better about her staying in his penthouse, knowing that she was safe because Hogan was back and guarding her.

And he almost said it.

But he remembered what it was like, feeling antsy and restless, knocking around four walls and desperately trying to find busywork to occupy his mind, even though it seemed like that had been eons ago now.

His eyes swept over Nadine and he realized that she was already dressed to go out, so he couldn't use that as an excuse to turn her down. He couldn't say that he didn't have time to wait for her to get ready because she already *was* ready.

Who knew? Maybe she would pick up on something that might elude him?

He decided that it wouldn't hurt anything to take her with him.

"Okay," he told her.

"Okay?" she repeated almost numbly, afraid to let herself believe that she had won him over so easily.

There had to be a catch, some condition she had to meet before he actually agreed that she could come along with him.

She waited for the hammer to drop. But all Caleb said was, "Okay, you can come with me to prison. Just let me make a couple of calls to get us around some of the procedures you usually need to go through."

"You make it sound so romantic. You really know how to treat a woman," Nadine told him, trying her best not to laugh.

He was really out of practice in that department, Caleb thought. He couldn't even remember the last time he had taken a woman out when it wasn't directly related to a case he was working.

"You're always free to stay here," he reminded her.

Afraid she had insulted him, she was quick to retrace her steps.

"No thank you, I'm coming with you." And then she looked at him curiously, asking, "Do you have to set a separate alarm for your sense of humor in the morning? What time does it normally get up?" she wanted to know.

"At the same time I do, wise guy."

"I'll take your word for it," Nadine responded. An afterthought hit her. "I'm going to leave the dishes in the sink for now. That way I won't hold you up. I'll just wash them when we get back," Nadine promised.

"You really don't have to," he reminded her, picking up his briefcase and making his way to the hall closet. "I've still got that dishwasher."

"Well, I wouldn't want to 'hurt' its feelings," she told him, her eyes sparkling. "I'll look into using the dishwasher once we come back again."

Caleb went to make his call. Fifteen minutes later, he was back. "All set," he announced. Glancing at the sink, he saw that it was empty. She didn't waste any time, he thought.

Opening the closet, he took out his overcoat and put it on. The news had promised that today was going to be exceptionally cold and he had found that the weather bureau was rarely wrong when they gleefully predicted frigid conditions.

Leaving the coat unbuttoned, Caleb looked at her. She was still dressed in a tailored suit. "You're going to want to wear something over that," he suggested. "Like a winter coat."

Nadine glanced up the stairs. "It's in the closet in the room you told me to use."

At least she had thought to pack it. "So? Is there any reason why you don't go upstairs and get it?"

Nadine hesitated. There was a reason, all right,

but she was afraid if she said it out loud, she would be insulting him. Of course, if she didn't say it out loud, she could very well be left behind.

"Actually, yes," she finally admitted.

"I'm listening," Caleb told her.

Bracing herself, she said, "I'm afraid that if I dash upstairs to get my overcoat, you'll use that as an excuse to leave me behind and go."

He looked at her in surprise. "You actually think I'd do that?" he questioned. What kind of vibrations was he giving off? Caleb wondered.

"Well, you indicated that you would rather that I remained here, busying myself with making jewelry," she reminded him.

"I didn't quite put it that way. And I didn't mean to make it sound as if I didn't want you coming with me. I just didn't think that you would particularly want to come to prison with me."

"I find the nature of your work exciting," she said honestly. "And prison visits are just part of it."

Caleb looked at her thoughtfully. She was one unusual woman, he couldn't help thinking.

"Go get your winter coat," he told her, adding, "You've got five minutes."

Nadine was already racing up the stairs before the last words were out of his mouth.

Chapter 16

Caleb pulled his car into a space within the parking lot that was in front of the private prison where Ronald Spence was currently serving out his several life sentences.

Turning off the ignition, Caleb looked at Nadine. "Last chance to change your mind and wait in the car while I talk to Spence," he offered.

Nadine had been keenly aware of her surroundings for the last five minutes, taking absolutely everything in.

"Right now, I think I'd be safer with you than staying in the car," she told him honestly.

"There are security guards around," Caleb pointed

out, thinking that might make her feel more at ease and tip the scales in favor of remaining inside.

"I know," she answered. "But I'd still feel safer with you." She had caught a glimpse of one of the guards as they drove through the gate surrounding the prison. The grim-looking man did *not* look all that happy to be here.

"Okay, then stay close," Caleb said to her.

Nadine's mouth curved. "You don't have to tell me that twice," she responded.

As she continued to take in the atmosphere, Nadine found herself thinking that the facility left a lot to be desired.

Oh, it appeared to be clean enough, she judged, but there was something about the very air around it that left a rather less-than-savory impression of the place.

Walking through the prison's entrance to the desk, Caleb held up his identification for the main guard's benefit. Nadine quickly produced her own ID—her driver's license—and followed Caleb's example.

"We're here to see Ronald Spence," Caleb told the guard whose badge identified him as one D. Adams. "I called ahead to make the arrangements," he added.

The man looked over both of the IDs, lingering over Nadine's before finally nodding his head.

"Visitors have to register in the inmate visitation

system prior to having an appointment with the inmate," Adams told them.

When they completed the process and crossed the floor, he waved them over toward a row of haphazardly arranged chairs.

"Wait there," Adams ordered, then disappeared behind another door. Caleb could only presume that the head guard was going to bring back the prisoner.

"What a cheerful place," Nadine couldn't help commenting.

"Compared to some of the other places I've been to, this is positively paradise."

A few minutes went by before the head guard returned. Standing just beyond the doorway's threshold, Adams waved for them to come in. When they did, he ran a search wand over them, looking for any hidden weapons. Satisfied that they were clean, the man ordered, "Come this way." He was looking at Caleb as he said it.

Caleb complied, pausing to glance over his shoulder to make sure that Nadine was following behind him. She was, so he continued walking behind the guard.

They went down a long, winding narrow hallway with several gates, which eventually opened up to what appeared to be a communal visiting area for inmates and their families.

Looking at it, Nadine felt a chill working its way up and down her spine.

"Take a seat," Adams told them gruffly, gesturing toward what appeared to be an abundance of empty tables. There were obviously not too many visitors here today. "I'll bring the prisoner out."

Due to the number of times she had been arrested herself during protest demonstrations that had gotten out of hand, Nadine was used to the way that prisoners and potential inmates were impersonalized by the guards. But she still found it rather disconcerting to hear.

Adams returned quicker this time, bringing with him a man who appeared to be rather unaffected by the living conditions around him.

Ronald Spence looked to be about of average height and medium build. Once he came closer, Nadine realized that he looked like a man who was struggling to hang on to the last vestiges of hope.

"You've got ten minutes," Adams told Caleb before he withdrew to the far end of the large room. Nadine noticed that the dour-faced guard took a post by the door, facing them and watching every move that Caleb, the prisoner and she made.

Even from across the room, Nadine couldn't help thinking Adams gave the impression of a man who didn't trust anyone.

Meanwhile, Spence was busy sizing up the man

who had finally come to see him. "You're Ben Colton's son." It wasn't a question; it was a conclusion.

Caleb put his hand out toward the prisoner. "I am."

Spence nodded, more to himself than to Caleb. "You look like him," he said. Belatedly, Spence held out his hand toward Caleb's and shook it. And then his attention turned toward the only unidentified person at the table. He nodded toward Nadine. "Your assistant?" he asked Caleb.

Nadine spoke up before Caleb could answer. "Yes, I am," she said to the man they had come to see, thinking it was a lot simpler that way than telling Spence that Caleb had brought her along to keep her from going stir-crazy, which was what it actually boiled down to.

Spence's attention had already shifted back to Caleb. "I can't believe that you're finally here," the man said, looking at Caleb in disbelief. "I've called your office so many times, I was starting to think that I'd never get anyone to listen to me."

"Well, I'm here now and I'm listening," Caleb told him. "Why don't you tell me what happened in your own words?"

"It's really simple. I know you probably think I sound like every other prisoner who has ever been convicted and incarcerated, but I am innocent," Spence stressed with passion before getting down to the heart of the matter. "I just recently found out that the evidence that would have cleared me of the charges that were leveled against me was deliberately hidden by Judge Colton."

Spence couldn't keep the anger and sense of betrayal out of his voice.

Caught up in the drama, Nadine spoke up. "Where is this evidence?" she wanted to know, then flashed Caleb an apologetic look for speaking out of turn.

"I don't know where it is," Spence complained, visibly frustrated. "If I knew where, I would have found a way to get my hands on it." He looked at Caleb, remaining, Caleb noted, as calm as he could under the circumstances. "Will you do it? Will you take on my case? The word is that you and your sister are trying to do right by all those people your father unjustly sent away so he could line his pockets and live the high life." Spence looked at Caleb as if his last shred of barely contained hope was seeping from his very being.

"My firm's working several other cases at the moment. But give me all the information you can, including letters in your possession that I might be able to use in your case, and I'll see what I can do."

Spence nodded, then said to the son of the man who had sent him into this prison, "Don't just 'see,'" he told Caleb. *"Do,"* he all but pleaded.

The last man that Ben Colton had sent away to

prison went on to tell his visitors where they could find the papers that could at least point them in the right direction. He had placed the documents in a safety-deposit box that was in his ex-wife's name.

Taking all the information down, Caleb promised to do what he could for Spence. This was the last person his father had put away. Despite currently having several other cases to work on, this was a point of honor for Caleb. Maybe even an obsession, he allowed, but he felt he owed it to Spence.

They left the prison shortly after that. Despite the initial restriction that Adams had issued, their visiting time had been mysteriously stretched by an extra five minutes on top of the initial ten.

Adams said nothing when he saw them, he merely pointed toward the exit, indicating that they should leave. Caleb and Nadine gladly complied.

"So, what do you think?" Caleb asked as they made their way back out to the prison's exit.

"You're asking my opinion?" Nadine had to admit that she was surprised by that.

"That's why I decided to bring you," Caleb answered.

She still didn't quite get it. "Why? Because of my numerous arrests?" She couldn't think of any other explanation.

Caleb frowned slightly. "Because of your gut instincts, dealing with people on the other side of the arresting officer, as an activist," he told her.

"All right," Nadine said, accepting his explanation. Taking a deep breath, she added, "My first guess is that Spence is telling the truth—either that," she amended, "or the man's an expert liar."

Caleb laughed as he shook his head. "You're waffling."

Yes, she was, Nadine thought. But then, he had asked her opinion, and besides, that didn't necessarily mean that he was going to take it once she gave it. One way or the other, Caleb was going to make up his own mind. She sensed that much about him.

"I really think," she told Caleb, "given your father's track record, Spence is being honest."

Caleb nodded. "Well, we're in agreement about that. Let's see if getting our hands on Spence's private papers is as easy as the man seemed to think."

Saying that, Caleb drove to the address that Spence had given him in order to pay a visit to the former Mrs. Spence.

Holly Spence appeared to know that they were coming and was prepared for them. Caleb could only assume that Spence had gotten in contact with her the same way he had initially managed to keep calling his office.

"If you don't mind my asking," Nadine said once

they were escorted into the woman's modest apartment. "Since you seem as if you still really care about your ex-husband, why did you divorce him?"

Nadine avoided looking at Caleb, thinking she had probably overstepped her bounds. But when she did finally look his way, he nodded his approval. Hard as it was to believe, he thought, he and Nadine seemed to be on the same wavelength. And he found that undeniably attractive, no matter how much he tried to keep her at an emotional distance.

Holly brought them into the small living room. She sat down on the lone chair facing her floral sofa.

"That was Ronald's idea," she told Nadine. "When it looked as if he was going to be sent to prison, he didn't want to 'drag me down' with him, as he put it. I didn't want a divorce, but I didn't fight with him about it since he was already dealing with so much. That's why I reluctantly agreed."

Her brown eyes swept from one visitor to the other as passion swelled in her voice. "But I know in my heart that he's innocent," Holly insisted. She rose back to her feet, asking, "Can I get you some coffee?"

It was obviously a foregone conclusion to her that they were going to say yes, so the woman withdrew into her kitchen to get them both some coffee.

And something else.

The brief visit continued over some barely decent

coffee and some rather surprisingly bitter chocolate chip cookies. After they had managed to partake of both, Holly Spence then awarded Caleb temporary possession of her safety-deposit-box key.

Caleb knew that wasn't enough. "You're either going to have to accompany us to your bank, or I'm going to need a copy of your identification as well as a letter written by you allowing me access to the box," Caleb informed the woman.

Holly hesitated, regarding him skeptically. "Are you sure about that?"

"I'm afraid that I'm very sure," Caleb told the woman.

Holly blew out a rather loud breath. "Well, all right. I can't come with you," she said, offering no further explanation. "But I can certainly give you that letter and a picture of my license." Saying that, she switched gears and asked, "How long before you can get Ronald free?"

It was hard to speculate if any of this would even work, and he didn't want to string the woman along, but he needed to tell her something positive. He could see that she desperately needed it.

"The sooner I can get the contents of the safety-deposit box, the sooner I can get to work on investigating his claims," Caleb told her.

That seemed to be enough to satisfy Spence's former spouse. Nodding her head, she quickly went to comply with Caleb's requests.

Armed with the name and address of Holly Spence's bank, Caleb's next stop was to go there.

Less than ten minutes later, Caleb was parking his vehicle directly in front of the bank's entrance.

Nadine smiled as she got out of Caleb's car. "Your job is certainly more involved than I ever thought," she commented.

Caleb laughed under his breath as he opened the door for her. "You don't know the half of it," he said to Nadine.

As she moved by him, he caught a whiff of her perfume, something light, but at the same time arousing. For a moment, thoughts popped up in his head that had nothing to do with why they were here. He caught himself really wishing that this was a different time and place.

The next moment, he forced himself to focus on their tasks.

Once inside, Caleb approached the first unoccupied teller he saw.

"I need to get into safety-deposit box 3206," he told the young woman. "Do I see you about that?"

The woman offered him a spasmodic smile. "Of course, sir, but I will need to see some identification from you, plus since I'm assuming that your name isn't on the account, I will need to see a letter from the present owner of safety-deposit box number 3206."

Caleb handed the woman a photo of Holly's license, plus Holly's letter stating that she allowed him access to the box.

Another ten minutes went by before Caleb found himself in a tiny space, sequestered with the safety-deposit box as well as with Nadine. The space was so small, there was barely enough room for them to simultaneously take a deep breath. He fought the deep desire to pull her close to him, to protect her and to kiss her more intensely than he'd ever kissed anyone before... Her passion and drive for justice matched his own, he'd found; that was something he'd never expected to discover in a woman. But he had to resist...

Later, he promised himself.

"I'm glad you thought of bringing that letter from Mrs. Spence," Nadine told him. "Otherwise, they would have no choice but to go back to Holly and have her write one."

Caleb smiled. "This isn't my first rodeo."

Nadine looked about the tiny, enclosed space. "Good thing because I don't think a rodeo would fit in here."

They barely fit there, she thought. Nadine couldn't help wondering if the room was built with smaller people in mind. It was either that, or it was actually made for only one occupant, she decided. And there was enough room to press herself up against Caleb and do more than just open up that safety-deposit box… They could finally give the sparks that had been flying between them since they first met some oxygen and let them burst into flame.

Caleb opened the elongated safety-deposit box. He found several folders inside. Not wanting to miss anything and definitely not wanting to remain in the claustrophobic space for the length of time a proper examination took—even if it meant brushing up against Nadine's curves again and again— Caleb opted to bring the entire contents of the box back with him.

Shifting cautiously in the small enclosure, Caleb struggled to put all four folders into his briefcase.

After closing the safety-deposit-box lid, he took it as well as his briefcase with him as he tried to make his way out of the tiny space. Shifting in it caused him to bump against Nadine not once, but twice.

Each contact generated a sharp sliver of electricity that insisted on traveling through his body.

As well as hers, he thought, if that startled look on Nadine's face was any sort of indication that she had felt something.

Caleb debated between apologizing for the accidental contact or just pretending that the whole thing hadn't happened and that he hadn't noticed anything.

He decided to go with the former.

"Sorry," he murmured.

"Me, too," Nadine quickly responded, for once not looking into his eyes.

Caleb was tempted to ask her exactly what *she* was sorry about but decided that it was more prudent to let the matter go.

At least for now. Until he could get a handle on whatever it was between them, he had to keep his focus on the cases he was handling: Al Sutherland and Ronald Spence. No more, no less.

Chapter 17

Nadine was desperate to move on from the awkwardness that had been created between them. An awkwardness generated within the tiny cubicle at the bank when they brushed up against one another. Or had that been a genuine electricity flaring between them? An electricity like she had never experienced before but desperately wanted to give in to.

She searched for something—anything—noncommittal to say once they finally got back into Caleb's vehicle.

She buckled up. "I can help, you know," she told Caleb as he turned his key in the ignition.

"Help?" he questioned, pulling out of the parking space and onto the main road. "Help with what?"

"With whatever you're looking for in those papers you found at the bank. At the very least, I can sort through them and give you a summary of what each folder contains. That way," Nadine continued, "you're freed up to turn your attention toward something else." *To me, maybe. Or* us, she thought silently.

Rather than jump at the chance, the way she had expected him to, Caleb shook his head. "You don't have to do that."

Nadine had no intentions of being that easily dismissed. Shifting in her seat, she looked at him. "Think of it as my way of paying you back for what you're doing for me." Then, in case he was unclear about what she was referring to, she clarified what she was saying. "Helping me find a way to get the family plot back from Rutledge Oil—not to mention keeping me safe from said oil company," Nadine stressed. And then she got to the heart of the matter. "I'm sure I wouldn't be able to afford you under normal circumstances, but I am *not* a charity case, either." She refused to let him see her as someone to be pitied; she wanted him to see her for the equal that she was.

"I never said you were," he pointed out. Seeing that accepting help without some sort of return on her part didn't sit well with Nadine, he told her, "We'll work something out."

By then, he was pulling into his underground parking space.

"Yes, we will," she agreed very firmly. "You'll take me up on my offer."

This was becoming very familiar to him. "This is another one of those losing arguments I'm having with you, isn't it?" Caleb asked.

For once, he had to admit that he wasn't really that upset about the situation. Right now, he felt he could certainly use some help sorting through things. *Like how I really feel about this woman who barged into my life and has turned it upside down*, he mused silently.

"Depends on how long you're going to continue going around and around about my offer to help you, but yes," she freely admitted, "it is."

"We'll talk later," he promised her. "First, though, I'm going to order some takeout for us." Unbuckling his seat belt, he got out of his vehicle, then waited for her to follow suit. When she did, he locked his car, then asked, "What are you in the mood for?"

"Answers," Nadine told him without a moment's hesitation, then smiled as she added, "and pizza."

"Any particular kind? Pizza, not answers," Caleb clarified, walking toward the underground elevator that would lead them to the penthouse door.

Nadine shrugged. "Anything you like," she responded. "Again, I'm referring to the pizza, not to the answers."

Opening the door to his penthouse, Caleb walked in and placed a call to his favorite Italian establishment.

No sooner had he ended the call than there was someone at his door, ringing the bell.

Nadine caught his arm as Caleb started for the door. When he looked at her quizzically, she explained her hesitancy.

"I've heard of fast delivery, but that's really going over and above the call of duty," Nadine said. She knew she was being overly suspicious, but she just couldn't help it. "Maybe someone was just waiting for us to get back to the penthouse."

Caleb found her worrying to be rather sweet. "Don't worry. Hogan spelled Jacobson and is back watching the place," he reminded her.

"Are you sure?" Nadine asked, still holding on to his sleeve. He could feel the heat of her through his shirt fabric but did his best to block the sensation. "I didn't see him."

"That's the whole point," Caleb told her. "Hogan knows how to be invisible."

Striding toward the door, he glanced at the monitor on the wall and opened the door. He was pleased to find his sister Aubrey standing right in his doorway.

Two inches taller than Nadine, the curvy thirty-year-old blonde gave her oldest brother an annoyed look through her thick lenses as she strode into the foyer.

"About time you came back. I stopped by earlier, but that somber, dark shadow you have lurking around told me you weren't in." She put her hands on her hips. "Does that man ever smile?" Aubrey asked.

Shutting the door behind his sister, Caleb secured the lock.

"Not to my knowledge," he said glibly, turning back around. And then he paused to make the necessary introductions. "Aubrey, this is Nadine Sutherland. Nadine, this rather outspoken young woman is my sister Aubrey."

"Sutherland," Aubrey repeated, turning the name over in her head. "Is she any relation to your ex-wife?" she asked Caleb.

It was Nadine who answered her. "Annie Sutherland is my cousin. Your brother is helping me with a legal matter," she explained, then to make sure that Caleb's younger sister had all the information, Nadine went on to tell her, "My father is Al Sutherland. He's a rancher."

By now, Aubrey had taken a seat on the sofa in the living room. Her expression grew rather pensive at the revelation Nadine had just made. She looked intrigued.

Trying not to jump to any conclusions, Caleb's sister asked, "Is that the land that's adjacent to the Gemini Ranch?"

Caleb nodded. "It is." The next moment, he turned toward Nadine, answering her question before she even began to form it.

"Aubrey and her twin, Jasper, are the owners of the Gemini Ranch. We occasionally went trail riding, all of us, in that area when we were kids.

"Needless to say, those were much happier times," he said sadly. "Aubrey and Jasper pooled their money, bought the land and turned it into what quickly became a very successful, all-year-round dude ranch. They've got cattle drives in the summer and horses and cattle grazing there," he told Nadine. Then he added with great pride, "Aubrey and Jasper are doing very well with the ranch."

Aubrey waved her hand dismissively at Caleb's words. At the moment, she was focused on just one thing.

"Do you think that your dad would be willing to lease his land to us so that we could graze our cattle there?" Aubrey was doing her best to keep the mounting excitement out of her voice.

Nadine's mind was going a mile a minute. The very idea of putting her father's property to work this way would solve so many problems for him, she couldn't help thinking. Heaven knew that it would generate an income that he could definitely use. More than that, it would put an end to the idea of his having to do fracking on the land.

There was only one obstacle.

"What you're suggesting would be a godsend," Nadine told Caleb's sister honestly. "There's only one problem getting in the way right now."

Aubrey looked from her oldest brother to Annie's cousin.

"What is it?" she wanted to know, keeping her eye on the prize. "Is there anything I can do to help move things along?"

Caleb shook his head. "I'm afraid not. It seems that Sutherland's strip of land is extremely popular. Rutledge Oil got their hands on the fracking rights in a less-than-scrupulous way."

It was obvious that she wasn't following her brother. "What do you mean?" Aubrey asked.

"Right now, it looks like they tricked Nadine's father into giving up his claim to those rights for next to nothing. But we haven't accepted defeat yet," he was quick to tell his sister. "If we manage to turn this around, I'm confident that you and Jasper can come to terms with Nadine and her father."

He glanced toward Nadine to see if she had any objections to the solution he had just proposed.

Instead of raising objections, Nadine immediately voiced her support. "Oh, absolutely," she assured

Caleb's sister. What was it about this Colton family? They all had such kind and earnest attitudes and seemed uncommonly generous with their time—and eager to help her, too. Nadine felt her heart soften a bit at the prospect of her dad working with Caleb's sister; maybe they could see each other, even, after all this was over?

Aubrey rose from the sofa. "Well, you've certainly given me hope. If anyone can get your father's land back," she told Nadine, "it's my big brother. He might speak softly, but trust me, he definitely knows where the jugular vein is located."

"You can put the shovel down now, Aubrey," Caleb said to his sister. "There really is no need to bury her in snow. She has already decided to turn to me for help in the matter."

"But I'm not trying to snow her," Aubrey protested. "If anything, I'm understating the matter." She looked at Nadine. "When my father, to put it politely, was 'removed' from the bench, the scandal that followed was utterly devastating. A lesser man than Caleb would have packed up and moved away, but Caleb dug in and diligently started working on repairing the family's reputation, even though he and Morgan were just teens, going through college and then law school. He and Morgan focused on making it up to all the people—and the families of those people—that our father had wronged in his last ten years as a judge.

"Now, thanks to Caleb and Morgan, the family reputation has been slowly but surely restored. Partially anyway. And some of the people whose lives were irreparably damaged by our father are getting the justice he denied them all those years ago."

"Okay," Caleb announced, getting to his feet, "enough is enough, Aubrey. Off you go. I—we," he amended, glancing toward Nadine, "have work to get to." He felt his face heat despite himself as he contemplated what else he and Nadine could do when they were alone again...

As he said that, the doorbell rang. He took a guess as to who was on the other side of the door. "And that would be our dinner," he told his sister. "I'll call you once we make some headway in getting Mr. Sutherland's rights back," he promised.

Nadine had accompanied the departing woman to the front door as well. "It was really nice meeting you, Aubrey."

"Oh, same here," Nadine responded with enthusiasm.

Aubrey looked at both of them. "Good luck!"

Opening the door, she all but bumped into the delivery boy, a fresh-faced teenager who was still trying to coax a reasonable display of facial hair to grow on his pale complexion. So far, he had just managed to raise a little sparse fuzz.

Startled to see three people on the other side of the door, he needlessly announced in a high voice, "Pizza."

"Just in time," Caleb said, taking out his wallet. He gave the delivery boy the price of the pizza plus an extra ten on top of that. As an afterthought, as the delivery boy was retreating, Caleb looked toward Aubrey. "You're welcome to stay and have some with us," he told her, adding, "I ordered an extra-large pizza with three kinds of cheeses and three kinds of meat toppings."

Once the lid was raised, the scent from the pizza began to fill the air.

Aubrey looked longingly into the pizza box. "You know you're twisting my arm, don't you?"

Caleb grinned at her, bringing the box in. "I figured as much."

Aubrey looked toward Nadine. "I'll stay for a couple of slices," she said, qualifying her choice by adding, "if it's all right with you."

"I don't have any say in this," Nadine pointed out to Caleb's sister. "But sure, stay. Eat your fill," she added.

Aubrey laughed dryly. "That is physically impossible," she confessed. "I never reach that 'full' stage. We'll keep it at a couple of slices."

Moving around the kitchen as if she had been doing it for a long time rather than just for a couple of days, Nadine quickly took three plates from the cupboard and three glasses as well. She took out three cans of soda from the refrigerator, placed them beside the glasses and plates.

"Dinner is served," she announced cheerfully, waiting until Aubrey took a seat before she followed suit. Caleb sat down between them. As much as he wanted to be alone with Nadine, he simultaneously dreaded having to resist the attraction that had arisen between them. So he welcomed Aubrey's presence at their friendly dinner, observing silently how well Nadine connected with his little sister. *Almost as if she was meant to—* He cut off the thought and returned to his meal.

It didn't take long before the extra-large pizza disappeared completely.

"Maybe I should have ordered two," Caleb speculated out loud, looking at the empty box.

Nadine stared at him in disbelief. "Oh, please," she cried, shaking her head. "I can barely move as it is."

Pausing at the door, Aubrey turned toward Nadine and told her in all seriousness, "Remember, my offer still stands. The minute you figure out this situation for your father, I will pay you top dollar for the grazing rights."

Nadine remembered that Aubrey wasn't the sole owner of the dude ranch, though. "Don't you have to ask your partner first?" she asked.

"I was born five minutes before he was," she informed Nadine. "Jasper won't argue," she added confidently. "Besides, he wants to be able to have our cattle graze there as well."

Putting her hand on the doorknob, Aubrey pushed the door open. "Good luck again," she said, repeating the words she had uttered before they had invited her to stay for dinner. Flashing a smile that instantly warmed up the room, Aubrey added, "And I hope to see you soon," just before she left the penthouse.

Chapter 18

Nadine was eager to keep her promise to Caleb. Early the next morning, she began to slowly and carefully comb through the stack of papers that he had taken out of the former Mrs. Spence's safety-deposit box and brought home. She dove into the task wholeheartedly, realizing as she did so that she was attempting to focus solely on work and not on the way her body and Caleb's had brushed up against one another yesterday…

Initially, Caleb had to admit that he did feel a little guilty about placing this burden on Nadine's shoulders. But right now, he was spread even thinner than normal workwise, and he was well aware that there was no way he could juggle everything that had come under the heading of being "his" responsibility. It was just physically impossible.

So, when Nadine had stepped up and volunteered to go through the files, he gladly took her up on it. She was the perfect partner, he mused. No way would he say that aloud to her—or even so he could hear it.

"Have I told you how much I appreciate you doing this?" Caleb asked four days later. He'd just come home for the day—early for a change—and found that Nadine was still working on the papers. She'd been enjoying going through Spence's files and had even asked to take on more work. She was sitting more or less exactly where he had left her early that morning.

Nadine looked up and cocked her head, as if she was thinking his question over, then with a smile creeping over her lips, she shook her head, her dark hair flying about her cheeks.

"No, not today," she answered. "Go ahead, tell me," she coaxed. "I'm listening."

"I have to admit that I had my doubts when I took you on after you volunteered," Caleb confessed. "But happily, I was wrong. I've seen your summary notes," he explained when she raised a quizzical eyebrow. "You really turned out to be an asset." *An irre-*

sistible one, he thought to himself, his hands itching to stroke the brown locks framing her face.

He really didn't need to praise her, Nadine thought. "All I want to do is find something we can use against that awful oil company to knock the pins right out from under them," she told him honestly.

Caleb sat down on the edge of the chair, looking at the way that the papers were spread out. "You've been at this nonstop, haven't you?" he questioned. Most people would have wrapped up by now. But not Nadine. Yet another reason he was beginning to rely on her more than he should.

"I take bathroom breaks," Nadine answered cheerfully.

He glossed over her response. "What about those earrings you were working on when I brought you out here?" he questioned.

"Well, turns out that the woman who commissioned them is currently away on a vacation, so it looks like I have a few weeks to spare before I need to finish them," she told him. "And right now," she said, looking at the papers that were spread out on the table, "this is a lot more important."

Her comment made him smile warmly. "You know, I just realized that you can be just as obsessive about something as I am." *Maybe we'd be a good team in more ways than one*, he couldn't help but think.

Nadine inclined her head as she looked up at Caleb. "I'll take that as a compliment." she said to him.

"Considering the way my single-mindedness has affected my life over the years, I'm not entirely sure that it *can* be taken as a compliment," Caleb admitted. "But the one thing I am definitely sure of is that you need to leave yourself some time to eat."

"Pizza?" Nadine asked, thinking that was where he was going with this.

But Caleb shook his head, vetoing the suggestion.

"No, I think that going to a restaurant would be more in order in this case." He rose to his feet and crossed over to where the coats were hung up. "Get your coat," he told her, leaving no room for an argument. "My guess is that you've been at this all day, and you need to get some fresh air."

Nadine looked down at the pages on the table. Part of her hated leaving the papers like this. In her gut, she felt as if she was getting very close to something.

But Caleb was right, she thought. Besides, the man had more experience than she did in extensive legal matters like this. She felt that she needed to back away for a little while. Doing that would undoubtedly give her the fresh perspective that she needed right now.

"Yes, sir," Nadine responded, giving Caleb a "smart" salute as she got to her feet.

A little more than an hour and a half later, pleasantly full and in a renewed, positive frame of mind, Caleb and Nadine were on their way back from the homey restaurant where they had gone for an early dinner.

"You were right," Nadine said as she looked in Caleb's direction.

"I usually am," he responded glibly. "About anything in particular this time?" Caleb asked good-naturedly.

"About taking a break and eating out," she answered. "I needed that," Nadine admitted. "I feel great." She waited for him to respond. When he didn't, she asked, turning toward him, "What, no comment?"

It was at that point that she picked up on the tension that was suddenly riding in the vehicle with them.

Caleb was not easily spooked.

Instinctively, Nadine looked over her shoulder and then up into the rearview mirror.

She almost missed it.

And then she made out the shape of a silver sedan driving behind them. It looked vaguely familiar.

She had to be wrong, she thought nervously.

"What's up?" she asked. Nadine could feel herself bracing for his response even as the words emerged from her mouth.

He was not about to play games. He wanted her to

be prepared. "I think we're being followed," he told her, looking in his rearview mirror again.

Was it his imagination, or was that car speeding up? He pushed down on the gas pedal. "That silver sedan has been shadowing us ever since we left the restaurant."

"It's not a coincidence?" Even as Nadine asked the question, she knew what his answer was going to be.

"I don't think so. That's the same one that was following you when I decided to have you stay at my penthouse," he informed her, turning sharply. "I'm going to try to lose him."

She could feel the breath backing up in her lungs and her fingertips growing icy. Nadine refrained from saying anything. She didn't want to distract Caleb if she could help it.

Caleb picked up speed, trying to outrace the car that was following them, but the latter turned out to have a more powerful engine. Not only did it stay abreast of the vehicle that Caleb was driving, it was also steadily increasing velocity.

Any minute, it would be going neck and neck with him.

"Hang on," Caleb ordered, then employed every evasive maneuver that the former secret service agent had taught him.

It wasn't enough. No matter how fast he drove, the car that was following them drove faster. It looked like he just couldn't lose the other vehicle, which swerved close and almost hit them. Nadine swallowed a scream, digging her fingernails into the armrests.

And then, just like that, it abruptly took off as the sound of an approaching police siren suddenly pierced the air.

The siren grew louder and louder.

Caleb released the breath he realized he had suddenly sucked in. The relief he felt was completely overwhelming.

"Looks like the cavalry's here," he told her. Looking in her direction, Caleb was startled. Although his car had come to an abrupt stop he hadn't been counting on, he hadn't realized that Nadine had been hurt until he saw the gash on her forehead.

She was bleeding from what looked to be a four-inch cut. He realized that she had to have hit her head against the dashboard when the car swerved and he came to an abrupt stop.

So much for thinking he could protect her, Caleb angrily upbraided himself. He shifted toward her as the siren grew louder.

"Nadine," he cried. "You're hurt."

She tried to wave off his concern, moving her hand weakly. "I'm okay," she said to him. Her words didn't exactly carry much conviction.

"No, you are not okay," he insisted. He took his

handkerchief out, wiping away the blood that was just above her eye, concern welling up inside him. He tamped it down so Nadine wouldn't panic. "See?" he asked, holding up the handkerchief for her to look at.

Nadine shrugged. "I bleed easily," she said dismissively.

He was still worried, though he admired her tough demeanor despite himself. "How many fingers am I holding up?" he wanted to know, raising his right hand up in front of her. He curled his thumb in front of his fingers.

"All of them," she answered, annoyed. At that moment, a police vehicle with dancing lights pulled up beside Caleb's car.

The gray-haired chief of police stepped out. Theodore Lawson was a tall, well-built man who looked younger than the eighty-one years that was written on his driver's license. He also acted younger. But at the moment, when he recognized both the car and who was driving it, the chief looked close to his age. He also appeared gravely concerned.

Looking into Caleb's car, Lawson motioned for him to lower his window. When Caleb did, the chief immediately asked, "Are you two all right?"

"We're fine," Nadine answered a little too quickly and emphatically. From the way her voice sounded, the chief thought she really seemed to be in pain.

A very skeptical look passed over the chief's face.

"That gash on your forehead says otherwise," he told her. His eyes shifted toward Caleb. "But you're all right?" he asked as he looked Isa's eldest son over.

"I am," Caleb asserted. "But Nadine needs to be taken to the hospital to be checked out."

Nadine frowned at him. "No, I don't," she insisted. "I just need a Band-Aid."

"No," the chief of police contradicted, "you need to go to the hospital to get yourself looked at." And then he looked at Caleb. "You both do. Your mother would never forgive me if anything wound up happening to you as a result of this." As far as Lawson was concerned, that was the end of the argument. "You know who nearly ran you off the road?" he said as he looked from Caleb to the woman whom Caleb had referred to as Nadine.

"I have my suspicions," Caleb said to the chief. "But if you're asking me if I have a name for the individual, I don't."

Lawson nodded. "I'll take down anything you can tell me. And, if I were you, I'd invest in a dashboard camera," he told Caleb. "Hopefully, this is the end of it, but just in case it isn't, and there's a 'next time,' it wouldn't hurt to have one of those cameras recording whatever might happen."

Caleb nodded, thinking that was a good idea. "I'll definitely look into getting one."

The chief nodded. "Wait here. I'm going to radio for an ambulance."

"An ambulance?" Nadine echoed, dismayed. She looked at Caleb. "Can't we just drive there in your car?"

About to place the call, Lawson looked at Isa's oldest son. "Does she argue about everything?" he asked Caleb.

Caleb nodded. "Everything," he replied.

Lawson patted the younger man on his shoulder. "You have my sympathies, my boy," he told Caleb.

The chief added to Caleb, "I'm going to have to tell your mother about this."

Caleb frowned at that. "Is that really necessary? I don't remember hearing that was part of police protocol now," he said.

"No, it's not," Lawson admitted. The breeze had picked up and was ruffling his gray hair, causing it to annoyingly fall into his green eyes. He raked his fingers through it, attempting to push it back into place. "It's part of my attempting to maintain a cordial relationship with your mother," Lawson admitted.

Caleb looked intrigued. "I thought you two had gone past 'cordial' a long time ago," he told the chief.

Lawson laughed under his breath. "We haven't. Not for lack of my trying," he admitted. "Your mother seems to be under the impression that anything beyond a polite exchange of words on her part would be construed as being unfaithful to your father's memory."

It was obvious that the situation did not sit well with the never-married police chief. But Caleb knew Lawson had long been enamored with Isa and felt she was worth waiting for, no matter how long it took for her to come around.

Caleb shook his head. He was well aware of the way his mother felt about his late father. "She really is something else, isn't she?"

"Your mother is a lady," Lawson insisted. The chief evidently felt called upon to come to Isa's defense.

Caleb nodded. There was no disputing that, he thought. "My mother's lucky to have you."

The chief laughed again. "You might try to convince her of that."

Just then, the ambulance the chief had called for arrived. Nadine looked longingly at Caleb's vehicle. Despite the fact that it had been almost run off the road, it really didn't appear the worse for wear to her. She appreciated his concern—more than she really wanted to admit—but surely a small cut on the head wasn't worth all this fuss?

She was also worried about the vehicle being left behind. "What if that animal who followed us comes back and tries to do something to your car?" she asked. "Like maybe rigging it to blow up?"

Caleb looked at her in surprise. He had to admit that hadn't occurred to him. "You're just full of warm thoughts, aren't you?"

"It can happen," Nadine insisted. She wouldn't put anything past the driver she assumed was the oil company's henchman.

"I'll have one of my men drive it over to the hospital for you, so when you're ready to leave, you can," Lawson said, doing his best to reassure Nadine. "And," he continued, "until you are, I'll have the deputy stay with the car and keep an eye on it. Can't have you and one of Blue Larkspur's foremost attorneys meet with an accident as you're driving to his home," he said to Nadine. He smiled as his eyes met hers. "Feel better?" he asked.

"I will once you find whoever did this," Nadine told the chief in no uncertain terms.

"I'm working on it," Lawson promised.

He sounded so serious, Nadine was almost tempted to believe the man. But at bottom, she was a realist and knew that she and Caleb were not his exclusive concern. Crime wasn't exactly rampaging through the town, but the chief surely had more than enough to keep him busy.

The EMTs tried their best to get Nadine to agree to lie down on the gurney—but to no avail.

"I'll sit up, if you don't mind," she informed the

attendants firmly. Then, to convince the two men, she said, "If I lie down, my head will start spinning."

"How do you know?" Caleb challenged. "You haven't tried to lie down yet."

Nadine looked directly at Caleb, annoyed that he had raised the point.

"I just know," she said to him.

Caleb heard Lawson chuckle to himself. When he looked back at the chief, Lawson said, "I thought you were kidding before, but she really does argue about everything, doesn't she?"

"That's not something that I would kid about," he informed the police chief seriously. And then Caleb turned his attention toward the attendant who had climbed into the back to stay with Nadine. "I'm going to get in back with her," Caleb told the EMT, "if that's all right with you."

The attendant, whose identification tag proclaimed his name to be Matt, gestured into the ambulance. "Be my guest," he told Caleb.

Still very concerned about Nadine's condition, Caleb climbed into the vehicle and sat down beside her, taking her hand in his.

She didn't pull it away.

Both gestures spoke volumes.

Chapter 19

When Nadine finally walked into the penthouse just ahead of Caleb, she was more than a little relieved.

"I think I've had more tests done tonight than I've had done before in my whole life," she told Caleb.

She and Caleb had just spent the last three hours in the emergency room. She sincerely doubted that there was a part of her that hadn't been poked or prodded or thoroughly checked out from head to foot.

Happy to be in familiar surroundings, Nadine turned around to look at Caleb.

"Why the long face?" she asked. "There was no sign of a concussion, no evidence of internal bleeding or any sort of damage of any kind. Nothing," she declared. "Aside from that ugly cut on my forehead, the doctors couldn't find anything to even be concerned about. And heaven knows that they certainly did try," she stressed. "So I'll ask you again—" Nadine pinned him with a look "—why the long face?"

Caleb thought of just brushing her question off, telling her she was just imagining things, but he decided not to. The time for hiding his feelings was over, now that they'd had a near-death experience and he could have lost her before he'd ever really had her in his life.

"Because all I could think of," Caleb admitted solemnly, attempting to suppress all sorts of thoughts that insisted on crowding in his brain, "is what *could* have happened." When she still looked at him curiously, he stressed, "You could have been killed."

"But I wasn't," Nadine pointed out as she took a seat on the sofa. Even though she wouldn't admit it to him, her legs did feel a little wobbly.

"But you *could* have been," Caleb repeated, doing his best to try to keep his feelings from registering on his face. He took a seat on the sofa beside her.

She looked at him, completely taken aback by what he had just said and by the way that thought made him look so concerned, despite his efforts to the contrary. His brow was furrowed.

"You're really serious, aren't you?" Nadine asked.

Of course he was serious, Caleb thought. To his way of thinking, he had just found her. He wasn't ready to lose her yet.

Perhaps not ever.

Those words were drumming through his brain in what amounted to a staccato beat, but he still refused to allow them to emerge from his lips.

Experience had taught him not to put himself out there like that.

Nadine drew closer to him. She found herself in the very odd position of trying to comfort Caleb, despite the fact that she had been the one who had received the worst of it. After all, she had been the one who had gotten banged around in the car accident.

Still, her heart went out to him in ways that she knew it shouldn't.

"I'm okay, Caleb," she assured him in a quiet, soothing voice.

When he continued to look distressed, Nadine brushed her lips against his cheek.

And then something clicked.

How that casual contact wound up turning into a full-fledged kiss soon after, she really wasn't able to say. Maybe Caleb had turned his head at the wrong moment—or perhaps the right moment—but Nadine didn't know. What Nadine *did* know for certain was that it happened.

And when it did, happiness leaped up inside her.

Nadine suddenly felt as if there was an entire one-hundred-piece orchestra playing within her.

Moreover, the attraction toward Caleb that she'd kept telling herself she wasn't feeling succeeded in making a liar out of her. Just like that, it suddenly seized possession of her entire being.

Before she knew it, Nadine was leaning into him, turning a simple kiss into something a great deal more as she wrapped her arms around Caleb's neck.

The moment that their lips met, all the restraints Caleb had been trying to convince himself were in place completely evaporated, disappearing like mist into the hot air.

There were no more restraints; there was only desire, desire bursting out and completely covering all of him.

Caleb shifted even closer to Nadine on the sofa, pulling her onto his lap as he continued kissing her over and over.

Each passionate touch only grew in its intensity, feeding the hunger within him rather than managing to satisfy it.

Caleb hardly recognized himself. He did know that he hadn't felt like this in years—perhaps not ever, he amended as he attempted to reevaluate what was happening to him.

The thought made him draw back and look at Nadine. They had both just gone through a near-death experience.

Maybe he was going too fast, Caleb warned himself. He didn't want his own reaction and the anxiety that had been generated by it to overwhelm her.

With effort, he told Nadine, "If you want me to stop, I will."

She realized that she had felt an attraction sizzling between them almost from the very beginning. Nadine had tried her best to deny it by putting up roadblocks. But she now recognized those self-imposed impediments for what they were: just excuses to keep herself from falling for the handsome attorney wholeheartedly.

But the moment he had kissed her with such feeling, the excuses she was attempting to sell herself completely fell apart, disintegrating like a papier-mâché wall being hit by a hammer. She had nothing to hide behind, nothing to use as a shield except the words he had just uttered.

But she couldn't seek refuge there, either, because they weren't true.

"No," she answered in a sincere whisper. "I don't want you to stop."

It was as if some sort of signal had just gone off. He was no longer the man he had just been, but the man he was on his way to becoming.

A man who was more than eager to make love with her.

Nadine could feel her heart slamming hard against her chest as Caleb embraced her over and over again. Although his very being felt possessed by an eagerness that made him want to divest her of all her clothing in one swift motion, Caleb forced himself to go slowly for two reasons. He didn't want to frighten her, and he wanted to savor every moment.

A more leisurely pace would heighten that delicious sensation.

As he slowly drew her clothing, piece by piece, away from her body, Caleb kissed every new, uncovered area. His overwhelming excitement kept increasing with each passing moment.

Unable to remain a passive recipient any longer, Nadine began to eagerly pull at his clothing, unbuttoning, unzipping and drawing each piece off him. She felt desire and anticipation growing. She was impatient to feel his skin against her own, impatient to experience that heightened sensation as she stripped Caleb's surprisingly sculpted frame bare.

Nadine spread her hands along his body, absorbing the arousing sensation that very act created within her.

And then they found themselves both nude in each other's arms, awaiting the ultimate excitement that waited for them at the end of the road.

Yet they both still wanted the wondrous journey to continue at least a little while longer.

Caleb gently pushed her back onto the sofa, then proceeded to weave a web of warm, openmouthed kisses all along her body. And little by little, he went farther and farther down that same body, causing electricity to shoot all through her.

Nadine thought she knew was what coming, but when it finally did, she discovered that she didn't.

She could barely contain herself.

The explosions that seized her body and shot through it only managed to grow in magnitude and intensity.

Nadine bit her lower lip to keep from crying out. Having Hogan or one of Caleb's other investigators come breaking in to save them from what they could only imagine was some sort of impending danger would be a terrible way to bring this delicious episode to an end.

So she struggled to remain silent. Breathing hard, Nadine bucked and moved, absorbing every wonderful nuance that was being created within her, while still needing more.

Finally exhausted, she fell back on the sofa, trying to pull herself together.

Caleb was just about to bring the dance they were doing to its logical conclusion when she surprised him and suddenly, with renewed energy, reversed their positions.

She managed to flip him over and then straddled him, pinning him down in a sexy, dominant stance.

"What are you up to?" Caleb asked, both amusement and arousal highlighting his face.

"Shh," was all Nadine said.

Her eyes on his, she ran her hand along the most intimate parts of his body, glorying in the look that came over his face as she slowly worked the magic on him that he had so recently performed on her. She deftly used her fingers, and when she had managed to sufficiently prime him, she resorted to using her tongue.

The moan that Caleb emitted told her that she had gone about the task correctly.

He seized Nadine by her shoulders, drawing her to him. With a swift movement, he reversed their positions a second time. And then, his mouth pressed to hers, Caleb slowly entered her, sealing their union.

With slow, deliberate and methodical thrusts, he began to move. With each movement, the intensity of what was happening between them increased until they found themselves racing to that incredible pinnacle at the top of the summit that was waiting for them.

Hearts pounding when they finally reached it, they then plummeted over the edge, savoring the intense sensation seizing them both.

They found themselves wrapped in a wondrous euphoria that took them prisoner, holding them in its grip for what felt like an eternity. But eventually, they found themselves reluctantly slipping back to earth.

Very slowly, Nadine opened her eyes, then turned her head to look at the man who'd slid down to lie beside her. She found that the room was now darker than the inside of midnight. That was when she realized that they had forgotten to turn on the light when they had walked in. Their attention had been so focused on one another that they hadn't even noticed.

As she went to sit up, Nadine felt Caleb's hand on her shoulder, holding her in place.

"Where are you going?" he asked her softly.

"I was just going to turn on the light," Nadine explained.

"Leave it off," he told her. "Just for a moment longer."

Nadine could feel the corner of her eyes crinkle as she smiled. "I take it you're not afraid of the dark?" she teased.

"Some of the nicest things can happen in the dark," Caleb said. And then he turned into her, their nude bodies pressed against one another again. "Would you like to go upstairs?" he asked her.

"Why, Mr. Colton." She was close enough to Caleb for him to see her batting her eyelashes at him. "Are you trying to lure me into your bed?" she asked, a coquettish lilt to her voice.

Caleb laughed as he pressed a kiss above her cheek. "I might be." And then, in all seriousness, he felt he had to admit this, "You really gave me a hell of a scare today."

"Why?" she asked him innocently. "Was I too rough making love with you?" She was doing her best to sound serious.

To him, though, this was nothing to joke about. "You know what I mean."

"Yes, I know what you mean," she answered seriously. "And the accident wasn't my fault. If you really want to get technical, you were the one who was driving. Very skillfully, I might point out," she said. "Because if you hadn't been, we might have wound up a lot worse off than we did."

Amused, Caleb shook his head. "I'll say one thing about you. You certainly keep me up on my toes."

Her eyebrows drew together as she pretended to study him. "Is that the best thing you can say about me?" she wanted to know.

"Honestly?" he asked. "I'm better when it comes to showing what I mean than talking about it."

"That's a pretty overwhelming admission coming from a lawyer," she informed him, pretending to be surprised.

"Hush," Caleb told her.

Taking her hand, he rose to his feet and drew her up with him.

"Are we going somewhere?" she questioned.

A little moonlight had spread its fingers through the room, enabling Caleb to see the innocent expression on her face.

"Yes," he answered, saying, "I'm taking you upstairs."

"Oh? And what are you planning to do once we get up there?" Nadine asked.

"Well," he continued playfully, "if you haven't guessed, I'm planning on having my way with you again."

Her eyes sparkled. "Okay. As long as I know," she said.

Caleb approached the winding staircase, pausing at the bottom. "Any objections?" he wanted to know.

"Can't think of a single one—as long as you're not too tired," she qualified, laughing.

"I'm not too tired," he said to her, then, a smile still playing on his lips, promised, "I'll let you know when I am."

Opening the door to his room, Caleb surprised her by scooping her up in his arms and then carrying her inside. Once in the room, he gently laid Nadine on the bed.

Doubling back for a moment, Caleb switched on the overhead lamp.

"Now you want the light on?" Nadine asked, pretending to be surprised.

"Yes. I don't want to miss a second of this," he told Nadine as he lay down on the bed beside her.

They proceeded to make love with each other as if this was their first time.

Caleb felt as if he couldn't get enough of her.

All he could think of was that, miraculously, he had been given a second chance to enjoy being with her. For a moment back there, when they had almost been run off the road, he had thought that was the end of it.

But it hadn't been.

He was not about to take that for granted.

Caleb made love with her like a man who had just been reborn.

And when they were finally done, breathing heavily in each other's arms, Caleb gave himself a few minutes—and then repeated the seduction a third time but at a far slower pace.

Like the previous two times, he allowed himself to savor every moment of the experience.

The refrain that kept reminding Caleb that he had almost lost her continued to beat through his head until he reached the point that he was far too exhausted to think of anything at all, even that.

Putting his arms around Nadine, Caleb continued to hold her close to him until they both finally fell asleep that way.

Chapter 20

Caleb woke up to find himself alone in his bed.

Not knowing what to think—had he ultimately been too aggressive and driven Nadine away when she'd had a chance to rethink what had happened in the light of day?—Caleb quickly grabbed a pair of pants and pulled them on. Barefoot and holding a shirt in his hands, he was just about to go looking for her when Nadine walked into his bedroom.

She was carrying a tray with breakfast and a cup of coffee on it.

"Good morning, sleepyhead," she said, greeting Caleb with a huge smile that made his stomach do flips. "I thought you might like to have some coffee, toast and scrambled eggs before we get started."

Sitting back down on the bed, Caleb made room for the tray that Nadine set down.

"'Get started'?" he echoed, curious. He noticed that, unlike him, Nadine was fully dressed. And, unless he missed his guess, he could detect the scent of shampoo in her hair. Had she already gotten on with her day because she regretted getting involved with him?

She nodded, sitting on the edge of his bed. "With the investigation," she told him. "I would bet *anything* that the guy who tried to run us off the road last night was someone working for the oil company. That can only mean one thing. That I've—that *we've* become a thorn in Rutledge Oil's side, trying to get them to admit that they stole my father's land.

"We need to find out what they're trying to hide," she concluded, her voice gaining in volume and momentum. He admired her passion.

"By the way, when I was sifting through the papers that I am going to be reviewing today, I noticed that you're also working on a case that's attempting to free a woman who was wrongfully convicted and imprisoned." Admiration shone in Nadine's eyes as she looked at him. "You really are a crusader, aren't you?"

Caleb shrugged off the compliment although his heart warmed at hearing her speak those words. It wasn't his way to bask in things like that. Praise had never been his end goal. Success was.

"I do my part," he replied modestly.

"Oh, you do more than that," Nadine said. "You put yourself out there when there's no real promise of any sort of actual monetary reward," she stressed. "I happen to think that's extremely noble of you." She grinned at him, hoping her admiration for him genuinely shone through.

About to brush off the compliment that Caleb sensed was coming, he abruptly stopped as her words sank in. "Just how much did you read?" he wanted to know.

"Enough," was all that Nadine said. She looked down at the plate on his tray. "Finish eating," she coaxed as she got off the bed. "I'll be downstairs, working."

Caleb watched her leave, feeling slightly bowled over. Nadine had just let him know that she found the work he did not just interesting, but actually, to use her word, *noble*. None of the women he had interacted with in his life had *ever* said anything that even came close to expressing such an emotion.

For that matter, none of the women outside his family he interacted with personally had ever even expressed an interest in these cases.

Yet Nadine just had.

Who would have ever thought? Caleb found himself musing. But he could have imagined it. Both he and Nadine were big on helping underdogs and getting justice for themselves and others. *Almost like we're the perfect fit...* He shut down that idea before it could even finish developing.

Finished eating, Caleb quickly put on the shirt he had grabbed earlier, then slipped on a pair of socks and shoes. He hurried down the stairs carrying the tray that Nadine had prepared for him.

He found her working in his office.

Somehow, Caleb thought as he put aside the tray he had just brought down, she looked right at home sitting there, going through the pertinent files. As if she belonged...

Nadine barely glanced up as Caleb took a seat on the other side of his desk. Instead, she slid over a stack of papers and placed them in front of him.

"Take a look at these," she suggested. "I think that some of those pages might help provide the evidence you're looking for."

They had been working in his office for a while now—Nadine had honestly lost track of time—when the doorbell suddenly rang, shattering the silence. Nadine's attention was instantly focused on whoever must be standing there, waiting for them both.

It occurred to Caleb that she looked not unlike a

deer caught in the headlights of an oncoming vehicle. The color had drained from her face.

Why?

"Relax," he said to Nadine warmly. "If that was anyone to worry about, the men working for me would have stopped whoever had driven up to the penthouse and held that person until I had a chance to identify him or her."

Getting up, he crossed the floor and made his way to the front door.

Looking up at the monitor that was mounted on the wall beside, he laughed when he saw who was outside.

"No need to worry," he told Nadine. "It's just Morgan."

The next moment, he was opening the door before Nadine could even respond to what he had just said.

Morgan burst in, her attention entirely riveted on her twin brother. Six inches shorter than Caleb, she still looked formidable as she grabbed both his arms.

"I just heard about what happened," she cried, her blue eyes traveling all over him, visually reassuring herself even as she asked, "Are you all right?"

"I'm fine, Morgan," he assured his sister. "Come on in," Caleb said, although the invitation was really after the fact.

Morgan didn't seem convinced. Nadine admired her obvious concern for her brother; she loved the

Colton clan's closeness. "Are you *sure* that you're all right? Why didn't you call me?" she demanded angrily. "I had to find out about the accident from the police chief," his twin complained. "Do you have any idea how that feels?"

"I'm sorry," he apologized. "I didn't call you because it was late and I didn't want you to worry. Nadine received the worst of it," Caleb told her, directing her attention to the other person in the room.

"Nadine?" Morgan questioned. Then, looking farther into the room, she realized who her brother was talking about. "Oh, Nadine. Sorry," she apologized. Her voice was polite but definitely rigid. "I didn't see you."

Her sharp eyes swept over the other woman, taking in every nuance. It was obvious that she had concluded that Nadine didn't look any the worse for wear. And then Morgan noticed the cut on the other woman's forehead.

It looked pretty fresh.

"Is that from…?" Morgan's voice trailed off as she indicated Nadine's forehead.

"Yes," Nadine answered self-consciously. "But it's no big deal."

Morgan slanted a glance toward her brother. "Well, it certainly sounds as if Caleb seems to think it's a big deal," the woman observed.

To Nadine, the other woman's tone sounded rather

dismissive. She could tell that Morgan was being protective of her brother and she could also tell that the other woman didn't exactly view her in the most positive light. Nadine felt her stomach flutter; she hadn't realized until now how much the approval of Caleb's family might mean to her.

Morgan turned her attention back to her brother. "Maybe you should just take a vacation, back away from everything for a while," she suggested.

What his sister was saying generated an incredulous response from Caleb. "When have you *ever* known me to back away from anything?" he queried. Especially now that he and Nadine...

"Maybe it's time you thought about doing it," Morgan suggested. She glanced at her watch. "I've got to get back to the office," she told him. "I just wanted to check that you were all right." She paused, looking her brother over from head to foot one final time. "You *are* all right, right?"

"Yes, Morgan," he answered patiently, "I am all right. And so is Nadine," Caleb deliberately added.

"Nadine. Right," Morgan said, nodding her head as her eyes darted over toward the woman she felt had gotten her brother involved in all this to begin with. "I'm glad you're all right," she said to Nadine stiffly.

At the door, she placed her hand on her twin's forearm, securing his attention. "Call me if you need anything," she instructed. Then, as an afterthought, she turned toward Nadine and said, "You, too, Nadine."

Feeling really uncomfortable, Nadine forced herself to smile at Caleb's twin. "Thank you," she said, then added after a beat, just as the woman left, "I'll do my best not to bother you, Ms. Colton."

After he closed the door behind his departing twin, Caleb walked back into the office where he and Nadine had been working.

"Morgan worries too much," he commented.

Nadine was tempted to say something about getting frostbite from the exchange she had just had with his twin, but with effort, she kept her reaction to herself.

She felt that Caleb was probably oblivious to any negative vibes that his twin had given off. Which was why Nadine was taken completely by surprise when, out of the blue, Caleb suddenly said to her, "She can be a bit overprotective of anyone who gets close to her siblings."

Raising her eyes to his, Nadine said, "Excuse me?"

"Morgan," he said, nodding toward the door his twin had gone through when she left. "I know there are times that she can come across as being rather cold, but she doesn't mean anything by it," he assured Nadine. "Give her a little time," he urged.

Nadine shrugged, as if what had happened hadn't really hurt her feelings and made her defensive. She shouldn't really care what Morgan, a virtual stranger, thought, but she actually did.

"I can give her all the time in the world," she said.

He picked up on Nadine's tone. "She offended you, didn't she?" he asked.

Nadine fell back on a typical explanation, one she would have used to convince herself was the reason for the other woman's cold behavior—if she didn't believe otherwise. "Morgan was just being protective of you," she told Caleb.

"That's right," he agreed. "She was. But once she realizes that you're not a threat or trying to use me for your own 'nefarious' purposes," he added with a grin, "Morgan'll come around. I guarantee it."

Nadine looked at him. Was Caleb just talking hypothetically, or was he thinking of some long-range plan regarding their relationship? She didn't want to get too hopeful—she had been disappointed by men she'd dated in the past. And, quite honestly, it still wasn't clear to her if Morgan did or didn't view her as some sort of an invading threat.

Besides, compared to Caleb's sophisticated twin sister, she felt as if she was the embodiment of a country bumpkin.

"Nadine?" Caleb prodded when she didn't make any response to what he had just said.

Snapping out of the haze that the thoughts that were swirling through her head had created, Nadine nodded.

"Right. I'm sure Morgan will come around once she decides to approve of me."

How had Nadine come to that harsh conclusion, Caleb couldn't help wondering. "That's not what I said," he pointed out. "I meant when she gets to know you," he told her with a grin.

Lowering his eyes, Caleb got back to reviewing the paperwork that was still spread out in front of him.

Nadine pretended to do the same, but her mind was not on reading, or even on finding evidence against the oil company. Right now, what she was dealing with was all far more personal.

Last night had been truly magical, but who was she kidding, Nadine silently demanded. She was never going to blend in or be accepted by his family as anything more than just a friend.

Complicating everything was the fact that Caleb had once been married to her own relative. Annie being Annie, her cousin had always managed to have everyone react positively to her. That meant that his family had to have liked her. Which in turn meant that if she came on the scene in any capacity that remotely resembled being Caleb's girlfriend, she would probably be viewed as an interloper, even though

Caleb's marriage to Annie had long been over. Even Isa Colton would probably disapprove of them, she imagined.

Nadine felt herself growing depressed.

She was just asking for trouble, she thought, thinking she had a prayer of her relationship with Caleb ever taking off, or even of getting serious. He was unlike the type of guy she usually fell for—he was made for forever, not a fling, and what they had could never reach that stage.

If she had a brain in her head, Nadine told herself, she would back away before her heart was in danger of being completely trampled on.

Nadine was gun-shy. That sort of thing had happened to her far too many times.

She had a terrible tendency to fall for men who were all wrong for her. Men who, when all the chips were down, simply were not able to commit.

Nadine pressed her lips together, suppressing a sigh.

Eventually, she needed to act like an adult, Nadine knew, not like some lovesick child.

The only thing that was important here, she reminded herself, was finding a way to reclaim what rightfully belonged to her father. Not to fall in love with a man who would likely never feel the same about her.

"Nadine, is everything all right?" Caleb asked,

thinking that perhaps his sister's sudden, unexpected visit had managed to completely throw her off her game.

Nadine took a deep breath, centering herself before she nodded in the affirmative.

"Yes," she answered him, doing her best to cover up her preoccupation, "I was just thinking about how much I'm going to enjoy making the oil company eat crow."

"Did you find anything?" he asked, thinking that perhaps she had, given her optimism.

"No," Nadine answered. "But I will. I feel it in my bones."

He smiled. That sort of positive attitude would help them keep on going until they finally did find something, he thought. He admired her so much— her persistence, her optimism…

Caleb leaned over in his seat to brush a kiss on her lips. He was more than slightly surprised when she pulled back.

"No distractions," she told Caleb. "Not until one of us finds something."

Distractions.

He knew this refrain. It was code for his getting too caught up in his work again. He might as well face it. He was never going to change. It had cost him most of his adult relationships, and he was still at it. There was no reason for him to believe that he could change just because he was now on the edge of developing something with Nadine.

If he cared about her at all, Caleb admitted to himself, he would just back off and spare her the heartache that was looming over her just down the line. For both of them.

Chapter 21

Caleb glanced at Nadine, who was sitting across from him at the kitchen table. Her head was down and she was working.

Damn it, he thought, all he wanted to do was to take her into his arms and make passionate love with her.

Slowly.

What he really needed, Caleb decided, was to get away. To create some space between himself and Nadine so that he could clear his head. Right now, the desire for her he was experiencing was seriously clouding everything up, getting in the way of his thought process.

He couldn't work like this.

"I'm going to go to the office for a while," Caleb told her, getting up from the table.

"All right," Nadine responded. She was afraid to look at him, afraid he would see the desire she felt in her gaze and think of her as some sort of a lovesick puppy. And she did have to admit it to herself—she was falling in love with this man.

"I'm not sure how long I'm going to be," he went on to tell her.

She nodded, forcing herself to continue leafing through the file she had opened in order to avoid meeting his eyes.

It was happening already, she couldn't help thinking. Caleb was putting distance between them. Nadine could feel her heart twisting within her chest.

"I understand," she answered stoically, still not looking up.

"If you need anything, Hogan's here. You just need to buzz him," Caleb informed her. He knew he was lingering; still, he couldn't help himself.

Nadine nodded, but she went on to tell him, "I won't need anything."

"Well, in case you do, he's here," Caleb repeated. Placing a few things he needed into his briefcase, he headed for the door. "I'll see you later."

Nadine nodded, unseeingly shuffling papers just to have something to do with her hands. "Later," she echoed.

She didn't look up until she heard Caleb close the door behind him.

How could everything have just collapsed on itself like this so quickly, she couldn't help wondering. Reliving the last eighteen hours in her head, Nadine couldn't find any actual cause for the sudden change. Everything had been absolutely wonderful—and then it wasn't.

Maybe she had been expecting too much, Nadine told herself. After all, Caleb had all but run out of here. Maybe it had taken his twin coming on the scene to make him realize what a mistake he was making, allowing himself to make love with her. Or maybe—

Just then, her cell phone began to pulsate, intruding into her thoughts. Pulling the phone out of her back pocket, Nadine glanced at the screen. She could feel her disappointment all but consume her. She had really hoped that it was Caleb, calling her under some pretext, maybe even apologizing for having beat such a hasty retreat out of the penthouse.

But the number wasn't Caleb's.

It belonged to her father. He was calling her from his house. Not knowing just what to expect —would he even be lucid? Or would he be that vague human being who was making more and more appearances these days when she talked to him? She didn't know. She did know she had to answer the call.

"Hello?" she said a bit more loudly into the phone than she normally would so that he could hear her.

"Nadine?"

Her father sounded almost fearful as he said her name. At least he knew he was calling her, she thought. That was something.

"Yes, Dad," she answered patiently, "it's me."

"Help me."

Nadine instantly stiffened. There were all sorts of reasons why he had just said what he had. He could be asking her to help him with something as simple as making a meal.

Maybe he was—

Her mind instantly went to a dark place.

Trying not to sound panicky—instinctively feeling that would only make matters worse—she asked her father as cheerfully as she could, "Why do you need help, Dad?"

"There's someone in my house." His voice was barely above a whisper. "What do I do, Nadine? Tell me what to do."

He sounded like a helpless child, she thought, her heart almost breaking. In a very firm voice, she told him, "I want you to call the police, Dad. I'm on my way."

She heard a dial tone in her ear and could only hope her father was doing what she had instructed him to do.

Nadine grabbed her purse, taking out her car keys as she rushed out of the penthouse. She was glad that Caleb had had her car brought over and parked in his underground garage. She had an unnerving feeling that right now, every second counted.

Nadine sprinted to her car, sweaty hands pressing the fob. Pulling the driver's-side door open, she quickly got in.

The moment Nadine was behind the wheel and pulling out of the garage, she placed a call to Caleb.

Her impatience grew as every unanswered ring fed into the next one.

About to give up, Nadine became alert when she heard the phone finally being picked up on the fourth ring.

"Nadine?"

Caleb sounded almost uncertain, as if he couldn't really believe she was on the other end of the call he had just received.

Relief flooded through every part of her. Thank heavens she had managed to reach him.

"Caleb, my father just called. He said that there was someone in the house and he sounded really afraid," she blurted.

"Where are you?" Caleb wanted to know, and the way he asked her, it was obvious that he was worried about her. Her heart warmed despite the fear churning in her belly.

"Where do you *think* I am?" she responded. Not waiting for him to answer, she said, "I'm in the car, driving over to my father's house. I told him to call the police," she added before Caleb could start lecturing her.

"Good. Now I want you to turn around, go back to the penthouse and wait for me there," he instructed. "We'll go over to his place together. You know, he could just be imagining things," he said to her gently.

She knew that was a possibility, but her gut was telling her something else.

"But what if he's not?" she countered. "What if there really is someone in the house?" she challenged. "Caleb, if I turn around and go back to your house and something does happen to my father, I would never be able to forgive myself. *Never*," she emphasized.

"Nadine—" Caleb began, determined to make her listen to reason.

She knew Caleb was going to try to talk her out of this and she was *not* about to listen to him.

"No," Nadine answered in no uncertain terms. "I'm going," she told him just before she ended the call.

Nadine pushed down hard on the accelerator. She was traveling faster than the speed limit, but this was her father, and whatever it took to get to him in time, she felt that her breaking that law was justified. She would explain everything to the police if it wound up coming down to that.

Nadine's heart was all but firmly lodged in her throat by the time she pulled up in front of her father's house.

Her car had barely come to a full stop when she leaped out of the vehicle. Running up to the front door, she swiftly unlocked it and dashed inside.

"Dad?" Nadine called, her head spinning as she looked from side to side. "Dad, I'm here. Where are you, Dad? Dad, are you here? It's me, Nadine," she called out urgently.

Where was he?

In response, she heard a muffled voice answering her. "I'm down here, Nadine. Down in the basement."

She released a huge sigh. At least he was all right.

"Come back up," she urged.

"No," her father cried defiantly. "I can't. It's not safe."

"Yes, it is," she told him. "Please, Dad. You can come out now. Really."

"No, I can't. Come on down here," her father said to her, then added, "I think I hurt my leg trying to get away."

She closed her eyes, trying to gather strength. That trite old saying was right. When it rained, it really did pour.

Nadine carefully made her way toward the steep stairs that led into the basement.

"I'm coming, Dad," she called to him, then warned, "Don't attempt to come up on your own."

That was all she would need, to have her father injure himself while he was trying to come back upstairs.

Nadine was seriously tempted to just run down the stairs in order to reach him faster, but she was determined not to take any unnecessary chances. So instead, Nadine had her hand hovering over the banister as she made her way down—just in case.

Seeing her, he immediately drew closer to the bottom of the stairs, as if a part of him felt she could protect him. His eyes were wide as he raised them to look overhead—like he could actually see through the ceiling.

"Did you see anybody?" he asked her breathlessly, still whispering. His eyes were darting back and forth across the ceiling.

"No, Dad, I didn't," Nadine told him patiently. She was ready to believe that her father, with his overactive imagination, had just created the whole scenario about a home invasion in his head. Taking his hand in hers, she quietly urged, "Come on, Dad, let's get out of here."

With that, she began to lead her father toward the bottom of the stairs. That was when she heard the basement door being slammed shut.

Startled, Nadine could feel the sound reverberating in her chest. She knew that sound. Someone had just locked them in.

"See?" he cried, vindicated. "I wasn't just imagining things! There *is* someone in the house!"

Her mind began racing. There definitely *was* someone in the house.

Nadine led her father back toward the side of the basement where he had been crouching. She was hoping to find a way out.

But there were no windows to break or crawl through. This area of the basement hadn't changed in years. There was no way to get out. The wall looked completely solid.

Her father looked at her, breathing louder and louder as his fear continued to mount. "We're trapped down here, aren't we?" he cried.

"No, we're not," Nadine insisted, doing her best to calm him, despite her own growing anxiety. "The police are on their way." When he just stared at her, she asked, "You did call them, didn't you?"

Sutherland looked at his daughter, wide-eyed and befuddled. "I don't know," he cried. "Maybe I did."

Just then Nadine heard an odd noise directly above them. The noise was followed by a crackling.

Within moments, the smell of smoke began to work its way through the cracks and openings in the basement, permeating the air.

The house was on fire.

* * *

Driving as fast as his car was capable of going, Caleb could make out the flames shooting up into the sky before he was able to even draw close to the Sutherland house.

His heart froze.

When he reached the home, he could see a ring of police cars and fire trucks surrounding the all-but-crumbled building that was being eaten up by flames.

Nadine was in there!

He just knew it!

As if to underscore his suspicions, Caleb saw Nadine's car parked just short of the ring of fire.

His heart plummeted down to the pit of his stomach.

Nadine *was* inside the burning house.

Why hadn't she listened to him? Why couldn't she have been reasonable and waited for him to get there?

The question echoed in his brain over and over again, taunting him. What was wrong with her anyway? his mind demanded. Did she think she was some sort of a superhero, able to do things mere mortals couldn't?

Damn it, why had he left her? He loved her!

Feeling physically sick, Caleb drove his car as close to the burning building as he could. Then, abandoning the vehicle, he wove his way toward what was left of the burning building, even as it was being totally consumed by the flames.

Damn it, he had finally found the woman he had been looking for all of his life, someone who felt as passionately about her work as he did, and he was about to lose her because all sorts of logical thoughts had gotten in his way, immobilizing him and making him behave like some sort of programmed robot. He should have gone after her, after someone who had made him happier in an incredibly short time than he could recall being in a very long, long time.

"Hey, you can't go in there!" a burly firefighter yelled out, grabbing Caleb firmly by the shoulders.

Caleb managed to shrug off the other man. "The hell I can't! The woman I love is in there. Don't you understand? I have to rescue her!" he shouted.

"That's our job, son, not yours," an older fire chief told him. "Why don't you just let us do our job? We don't want to have to rescue you, too."

Caleb managed to shrug that man off as well. Pulling away, he looked at the fire chief defiantly.

"You don't understand," he argued. "I have to go get her. I *have* to," Caleb insisted, ready to run into the burning inferno right now, no matter what.

"Caleb?"

He froze when he heard Nadine's voice calling out to him.

Chapter 22

Turning toward the sound of the voice he could only pray that he had heard, Caleb couldn't believe his eyes. For a split second, he was convinced that he was actually hallucinating.

But then Nadine, tears shimmering in her eyes because of what had very nearly happened, threw herself into his arms, and Caleb knew that this was no hallucination. She was real.

Nadine was real. His feelings for her were real.

Holding her, Caleb ran his hands up and down her back, pressing her close to him as if that very act somehow reinforced her presence for him.

"I thought—I thought—" Unable to finish, he just held her, absorbing the feel of her and finding infinite comfort in the fact that she was alive. "I really thought that I had lost you," he finally managed to say. "How did you manage to get away?" Her escape from the burning building had been nothing short of a miracle to him.

Even from the corner of his eye, he could see that the entire house was a total loss. The very sound of the building collapsing into itself was still reverberating through the air.

"It was Dad," Nadine told him, a bit of wonder still evident in her voice. She looked back at the man who was even now being placed onto the gurney. "For some reason, he suddenly remembered that there was an old root cellar put in beneath the basement and that it led out a distance beyond the house."

Caleb became aware of the smell of smoke embedded in her hair, but he didn't care. He was just happy that she was alive and here. He held Nadine close to him, kissing her face and raining kisses on her hair.

Caleb felt simply overwhelmed that she was all right, and he was doing his best to deal with the very unnerving thought of what could have been if her father hadn't put in that root cellar or remembered its existence.

With one arm around Nadine's shoulder, Caleb guided her over to the ambulance. There was nothing but gratitude in his voice as he asked her father, "How are you doing, sir?"

From his head to his toes, Nadine's father looked as if he had gone one-on-one with a fire-breathing dragon and had somehow, just barely, managed to emerge the victor. His clothes were a sooty mess and they reeked of smoke, but the man was very much alive.

"I'll be a lot better once I get my hands on those guys from the freaking oil company who burned down my house," Al Sutherland proclaimed angrily. His usual vacant appearance was nowhere to be seen. He was utterly furious and indignant.

The EMT politely interrupted the two men. "We're going to have to take you to the hospital to be checked out, sir," the attendant told Sutherland.

Sutherland scowled. "I don't need no one fussing over me," he insisted, only to suddenly have a coughing fit. It was obvious that Nadine's father had managed to swallow more than his share of smoke as they made their way through the root cellar.

"You do need to get checked out, Dad," Nadine said. As he stopped coughing, she saw that her father was about to start arguing again, so she made the request personal, saying, "Do it for me." Her eyes met his. "I almost lost you today."

Al sighed rather dramatically, like a man who knew he didn't have a leg to stand on. "Okay, okay. For you. But you gotta come, too," he told his daughter.

"I'm all right, Dad," Nadine tried to assure her father. She had had her fill of hospitals after nearly being run off the road the other day. But this time, it was Caleb who spoke up.

"I think your father and I would feel a lot better if you went to the hospital, as well, and got checked out." He knew that he certainly would. "And, if you're okay," he went on, "they won't keep you."

She saw her going to the ER in a different light.

"I don't want to waste any more time," Nadine insisted. "We have to go after those people who set fire to the house before they do any more damage. They almost killed Dad and me. Who knows what they might wind up doing next time?" she cried. She was positive that the men who did this weren't going to accept that their targets were still alive and walking around.

"And we will, I promise," Caleb told her. "But right now, your dad needs to be checked out—and so do you."

She had already explained to him that she was all right. "But—" Nadine protested.

"You know I'm right," Caleb countered. "I'll follow the ambulance—I'll have one of my people come to take your car to the penthouse," he promised, then got back to the immediate subject. "Once the ER doctor gives you the high sign, we'll focus all our attention on making the oil company pay for what they did. Deal?" he asked.

Nadine sighed, knowing she had no choice. Especially if it meant getting her father to go to the hospital, since he wasn't too keen on it. And she knew Caleb was right, too—and his care warmed her heart.

"Deal," she murmured.

Turning, she climbed into the back of the ambulance, taking a seat next to her father's gurney.

Caleb closed and secured the doors behind her. Once again, he felt infinitely relieved that she had managed to escape injury and was alive.

The ER physician on duty—R. Rosenthal, according to his name tag—checked Nadine out very carefully after she gave her insurance and personal information upon arrival. He told her in no uncertain terms how lucky she had been to survive the fire and then he let her know that she could go.

"Your Dad, though," Rosenthal told her, "needs to be kept under observation for the next twelve hours or so, but I'm optimistic about his prognosis. However, because of his age, we just want to be super-cautious."

Nadine nodded, clearly relieved in both instances.

"That's wonderful," she said to the doctor. "Can I see my father? I'd like to say good-bye before I go.

I don't want him to think that I'm abandoning him," she explained.

"He's asleep right now," the ER physician stated. "Besides the smoke inhalation, he was somewhat agitated, so we gave him a sedative because he did need to rest. Most likely, he'll probably be out until morning."

Nadine nodded. "All right. Then that's when I'll be back," she replied.

Waiting off to the side, Caleb was about to say something to Nadine about taking her home when he heard his cell phone ringing. Pulling it out, he automatically checked the screen to see who was calling.

"I've got to take this," he told Nadine, putting a little distance between himself and her as well as the ER physician.

Caleb answered his phone, instructing the person on the other end, "Talk to me."

Nadine watched as Caleb moved just out of range so she was unable to hear his end of the conversation. She had no absolutely idea why, but something made her realize that this call was not just important, but directly related to what had just happened to her father and the house he was no longer able to live in.

As far as that went, Nadine thought, her father could stay with her in the loft for now. She was prepared to take things one step at a time.

Nadine continued watching Caleb's back, trying

to second-guess what was going on just by observing the tension in his back. She wasn't getting very far, despite her feelings for him.

Caleb ended the call and slipped the phone back in his pocket as he walked back over to Nadine. Dr. Rosenthal had left, but Nadine's attention was entirely riveted on Caleb.

"Who was just on the phone?" she asked. She knew Caleb was an important man in the community, but even so, Nadine thought that getting late-evening phone calls had to mean something out of the ordinary was going on.

Caleb didn't give her a direct answer immediately. Instead, what he did tell her was, "You won't have to worry about Rutledge Oil anymore."

That immediately set off her radar. She was shocked.

"Why?" Nadine asked. "Did something happen to them?" She knew she shouldn't let herself get carried away like this, but she couldn't help it. Glee and confusion flowed through her in equal measure as she barely kept herself from hugging Caleb.

"Let's get you checked out of here first so we can talk about the call I just got without being interrupted," Caleb told her.

The look on his face promised her that this was all going to be well worth it, so she kept her questions and her curiosity under wraps as a nurse wheeled her out and Caleb walked beside her.

Because of the late hour, the process of checking out went quickly. There was no one else ahead of her.

Once they were in the parking lot, Nadine got up and into Caleb's car. Settling in, she buckled up, turned toward Caleb and proceeded to repeat her initial question.

"Who was that calling you on your phone?"

He started up his car and pulled out of the near-empty parking lot. "That was one of my other investigators," he told her. "Brady O'Neill. O'Neill is a tech whiz," he added. "Once I realized that Rutledge's henchmen might not be content just trying to harass you, I instructed him to install a number of hidden monitors around your dad's place, like I have installed around the penthouse. Turns out that paid off," he informed her. He glanced at her face as he drove home, "We have our proof."

"Go on," she urged impatiently when Caleb paused for a moment to allow his words to sink in.

"It seems that these guys aren't overly bright. They were caught on camera setting fire to your father's house." He saw a whole collection of emotions and thoughts pass over her face. This was the mother lode, what they had been hoping to find, and he felt a warm sense of vindication for Nadine and Al. "I can only guess that they were doing it to put an end to the threat that your father—and you—posed by poking around into their dealings.

"Apparently, they were trying to eliminate you once and for all." The very idea of that had his complexion turning a very bright shade of red as his anger flared. "But now it looks like they're the ones who are going to be eliminated—once and for all."

Nadine immediately jumped to the only conclusion she could.

"Does this mean that Dad can get his rights back?" she wanted to know, hopefully crossing her fingers.

He had been dealing with human tragedies for close to two decades now. Caleb really enjoyed being the bearer of good news for a change—and he especially enjoyed delivering it to Nadine. "It does indeed."

Because they were stopped at a red light, Nadine took the opportunity to throw her arms around his neck and kiss him soundly. "It's finally over!"

"Yes, it is," he answered.

She hugged him even harder, then released him as the light turned green. "I don't know how to thank you."

Slanting a quick glance in her direction, he laughed. "Well, that was a good start," he told her.

She grinned up at him. "To be continued once we get to your penthouse," she promised. In response, she saw an unexpected sad look suddenly come over his face. "We don't have to continue once we get to your place," she admitted to him, having no idea how to read his expression. Even though she wanted nothing more than to admit to him how she felt and have him return those emotions…

"It's not that. I'd like nothing better than to continue this once we're behind closed doors, it's just that I want you to know how very sorry I am about you losing your family home." He knew seeing it burn down to the ground had to have been extremely painful for her. After all, this was the place where she had grown up.

"I'm sorry, too, but at least because of you, we'll be able to get those horrible guys who did this—and their boss," she stressed. "And then no one else opposing Rutledge Oil will *ever* have to go through this kind of awful pain again," she pointed out.

Leave it to Nadine to see things in the best possible light, Caleb thought. She didn't belabor what she had gone through; she just saw the good that came out of the whole thing. And that was the kind of person he knew he wanted to spend the rest of his life with. Hopefully, she felt the same way.

"What do you think about building something brand-new on that spot where your old house stood?" he asked her.

She thought for a moment. "I think that it's a wonderful idea," she told him honestly. "A house that's up-to-date and that my father won't look so lost in. He'll love it," she concluded.

Caleb drove his car into the underground garage. After parking it, he went around to the passenger side and, opening the door, he helped her out. *What a gentleman*, she mused.

"I'm fine," she informed him, not wanting any special treatment. She didn't know whether he wanted a future with her, so she refused to let him treat her like she wasn't an independent woman.

He brought his face down next to her ear. "Humor me. I almost lost you twice now," he reminded her. "Let me savor the fact that you're here."

Nadine laughed, her heart pounding. "Far be it from me not to allow you to savor," she teased. "But shouldn't we file a report with the chief and have him go after those two arsonists just to be on the safe side?" she asked.

He smiled at her. "Already done," he told her. "I instructed O'Neill to give the chief a copy of the video capturing those two would-be killers in the act. They are being picked up and arrested even as we speak," he said as he escorted her into his penthouse.

She looked at him in amazement. "No grass grows on you, does it?" she asked.

"Hasn't been known to yet," he answered Nadine, feeling his heart swell with affection.

Once they were inside the penthouse, Caleb

locked the door behind him, then turned to take her into his arms.

"You have no idea how relieved I am to be able to do this, that you're really all right," he told her. "That you're alive," he added, working his way past the lump in his throat.

"And here I thought that maybe you were getting tired of me," she replied.

He looked at her and realized that she was serious. "Are you kidding?"

"No," Nadine answered honestly, "I'm not."

"Why would you ever think that?" he asked her, stunned.

"Well, after Morgan left, I felt you thought that maybe you had just gotten carried away last night and realized that you needed to rethink the situation. A situation that you actually regretted," she added.

"The only thing I *needed* to do," he emphasized, "was to rethink my priorities. I'll keep investigating Ronald Spence's claims that he was innocent tomorrow—I won't forget them, but you come first. That was when I realized that nothing is more important to me than you." He stopped himself before he wound up overwhelming her. "Don't worry, I'm not rushing you. We're going to take this one day at a time," he promised. "And then, who knows?" he said with a hopeful lilt in his voice, letting it trail off.

Her mouth curved. "Who knows?" Nadine echoed,

confident now that she knew exactly what would follow. She knew they'd win over Morgan and the rest of the family, that they'd be able to smooth over any awkwardness that resulted from her being Annie's cousin. They were just that good together—and they both knew it.

"Tell you what," Caleb said after kissing Nadine long and hard, just as he'd been longing to since he had found her standing outside her destroyed childhood home. "Let's go upstairs so that we can continue this conversation in more comfortable surroundings."

"Let's." Nadine's eyes were shining as she agreed.

Standing on the step just above the one Caleb was currently on so that she was closer to his height, she placed her hands on his face, tilted it and brought her lips to his.

Eventually, they finally made it upstairs, where they continued their "discussion" at a far more gratifying pace—and whispers of "I love you" and plans for their future together permeated the bedroom.

* * * * *

Look out for the next book in The Coltons of Colorado

Snowed In With a Colton *by Lisa Childs*

available March 2022 from
Harlequin Romantic Suspense!

#2171 SNOWED IN WITH A COLTON
The Coltons of Colorado • by Lisa Childs

Certain her new guest at the dude ranch she co-owns is hiding something, Aubrey Colton fights her attraction to him. Luke Bishop is hiding something—his true identity: Luca Rossi, an Italian journalist on the run from the mob.

#2172 CAVANAUGH JUSTICE: THE BABY TRAIL
Cavanaugh Justice • by Marie Ferrarella

Brand-new police detective partners Korinna Kennedy and Brodie Cavanaugh investigate a missing infant case and uncover a complicated conspiracy while Korinna is slowly drawn into Brodie's life and family—causing her to reevaluate her priorities in life.

#2173 DANGER AT CLEARWATER CROSSING
Lost Legacy • by Colleen Thompson

After his beloved twins are returned from the grandparents who've held them for years, widowed resort owner Mac Hale-Walker finds his long-anticipated reunion threatened by a beautiful social worker sent to assess his fitness to parent—and a plot to forcibly separate him from his children forever.

#2174 TROUBLE IN BLUE
Heroes of the Pacific Northwest • by Beverly Long

Interim police chief Marcus Price is captivated by newcomer Erin McGarry, who has come to Knoware to help her sick sister. But he has his hands full with a string of robberies and a credible terrorist threat, and he's not confident that Erin didn't bring the danger to the small community or that either one of them will survive it.

SPECIAL EXCERPT FROM

✦ HARLEQUIN
ROMANTIC SUSPENSE

*Interim police chief Marcus Price is captivated by
newcomer Erin McGarry, who has come to Knoware
to help her sick sister. But he has his hands full with a
string of robberies and a credible terrorist threat, and
he's not confident that Erin didn't bring the danger to
the small community or that either one of them will
survive it.*

Read on for a sneak preview of
Trouble in Blue,
*the next thrilling romance in Beverly Long's
Heroes of the Pacific Northwest series!*

Marcus watched as she got to her feet. He was grateful to
see that she was steady.

"Can we have a minute?" Marcus asked Blade.

"Yeah. Hang on to her good arm," his friend replied.
Then he walked away, taking Dawson with him.

"What?" she asked, offering him a sweet smile.

"I'm going to find who did this. I promise you. And
you're going to be okay. Jamie Weathers is the best
emergency physician this side of the Colorado River.
Hell, this side of the Missouri River. He'll fix you up.
But don't leave the hospital until you hear from me. You
understand?"

"I got it," she said. "I'm going to be fine. It's all going to be fine. I barely had twenty bucks in my bag. He didn't even get my phone. I had that in my back pocket. Nor my keys. Those were in my hand. So he basically got nothing except the cash and my driver's license."

Things didn't matter. "You want me to let Brian and Morgan know?"

"Oh, God, no. Please don't do that." She looked panicked. "Morgan can't have stress right now. I'm grateful that her room is on the other side of the building. Otherwise, she could be watching this spectacle."

They would want to know. But it was her decision. And she was in pain. "Okay," he said, giving in easily.

"Thank you," she said.

"Go get fixed up. I'll talk to you soon."

She nodded.

"And, Erin…" he added.

"Yeah."

"I'm really glad that you're okay."

Don't miss
Trouble in Blue *by Beverly Long,*
available March 2022 wherever
Harlequin Romantic Suspense
books and ebooks are sold.

Harlequin.com

Love Harlequin romance?

DISCOVER.

Be the first to find out about promotions, news and exclusive content!

f Facebook.com/HarlequinBooks

🐦 Twitter.com/HarlequinBooks

📷 Instagram.com/HarlequinBooks

📌 Pinterest.com/HarlequinBooks

You Tube YouTube.com/HarlequinBooks

ReaderService.com

EXPLORE.

Sign up for the Harlequin e-newsletter and download a free book from any series at **TryHarlequin.com**

CONNECT.

Join our Harlequin community to share your thoughts and connect with other romance readers! **Facebook.com/groups/HarlequinConnection**

HARLEQUIN

Heartfelt or thrilling, passionate or uplifting—Harlequin is more than just happily-ever-after.

With twelve different series to choose from and new books available every month, you are sure to find stories that will move you, uplift you, inspire and delight you.